TRAIL OF THE SEAHAWKS

The Macaque Cycle, Book Two

A Novel of the Future

by

I0665006

Ardath Mayhar

and

Ron Fortier

The Borgo Press
An Imprint of Wildside Press LLC

MMVIII

Copyright © 1987, 2008 by Ardath Mayhar & Ron Fortier

All rights reserved.
No part of this book may be reproduced in any form
without the expressed written consent
of the author and publisher.
Printed in the United States of America

www.wildsidepress.com

FIRST WILDSIDE EDITION

CONTENTS

FOREWORD

Many years ago, Ron Fortier and I were exchanging letters, as we had made contact after I had a story published in a small magazine he read.

In time, we began playing with the notion of writing a book together, and the first of these was *Trail of the Seahawks*, which we completed in about six months, sending the material back and forth by snail mail, as the computer was still in our future.

When TSR accepted that book for publication, our editor wanted to know how the world reached the point at which it exists in this book. We consulted, by letter and by phone, and in time we produced *Monkey Station*, to fulfill that need.

We had great fun writing this story, and I still think it is great fun to read, as well.

—Ardath Mayhar
Chireno, Texas
May 2007

ABOUT THE AUTHORS

RON FORTIER has been writing professionally for the past thirty-five years. Besides fantasy adventure, he has written over 500 comic book titles and recently began a new series of novels featuring the classic pulp hero, *Captain Hazzard*. He lives in New Hampshire with his wife Valerie, has five kids and six grandchildren. You can catch up with him at his website (www.Airship27.com).

The author of sixty-two books, more than forty of them published commercially, **ARDATH MAYHAR** began her career in the early eighties with science fiction novels from Doubleday and TSR. Atheneum published several of her young adult and children's novels. Changing focus, she wrote westerns (as **Frank Cannon**) and mountain man novels (as **John Killdeer**). Four prehistoric Indian books under her own name came out from Berkley. Historical western *High Mountain Winter* was published by Berkley Books under the byline **Frances Hurst**.

Recently she has been working with on-line publishers. *A Road of Stars* was her first original novel to appear in print-on-demand format. Many of her out-of-print titles are now available from e-publishers fictionwise.com and rene-books.com; many other novels are being published by the Borgo Press Imprint of Wildside Press and Amazon.com.

Now in her seventies, Mayhar was widowed in 1999, after forty-one years of marriage, and has four grown sons. The bookshop she ran with her husband for fifteen years was closed after his death. She now works at home, writing short fiction and nonfiction, and doing book doctoring professionally. Her web pages can be found at: w2.netdot.com/ardathm/ and http://ofearna.us/books/mayhar.html.

PROLOGUE

The jungle was alive with subtle sounds, which were interrupted from time to time by the raucous squawks of one of the huge parrots, which sat like colorful tents, making branches sag dangerously beneath their weight. Nothing could move without rousing the interest and comments of the tenants of the trees.

Koo, waiting in the shade beside a tiny clearing, knew that he would hear the approach of anything—or anyone. If the parrots didn't warn him, the Small Brothers in the trees surely would. As he waited, he fingered the amulet around his hairy neck. He twitched his agile tail, curling its tip around a young tree or snaking it forth to admire its length and glossiness. His family had always prided themselves on their tails.

At a great distance, there was a sudden cacophony. The Small Brothers above him scampered through the treetop to discover what was happening along the Big Trail that ran beside the river, Koo didn't move. The meeting was to take place here.

He sighed impatiently. If this one he awaited could provide the information his people needed, life would change dramatically and permanently for the Macaque. They would leave the jungles of the south, where their ancestors had once been just such creatures as the Small Brothers in the trees. The strange plague, now a dim legend to these forest-dwellers, had, he understood, altered many living beings, changing them drastically.

For the Macaque, that change had included a growing restlessness, an increasing curiosity about the world outside

7

their own small corner of it.

A red and blue and gold parrot flapped gigantic wings, stirring the air even down where Koo was sitting. The bird uttered its nerve-shattering cry, and Koo stood to greet the one who came through the barrier of low growth.

It was a man, of course. He was far taller than Koo, who came only just above the man's waist in height. His long black hair was strained back into a knot, and his dark eyes were glancing alertly about the clearing. When he saw Koo, he relaxed a bit. After many years of mutual suspicion, Man and Macaque, here in the remote jungles, had come to trust one another to some extent.

The Macaque moved forward. He held up the amulet as a greeting and a reminder. In his turn, the Man fumbled at his waist and pulled from a fold of his skirt-like garment an intricately carved ornament, whose polished curves reflected the light beneath the high canopy of treetops.

"You have come. We of the Macaque are grateful," Koo waited for the formal reply.

"A favor received requires another in return. Our Brother was caught from the swollen river and returned to us. What may we offer to you in return for a life? That is a great gift." The Man, smiling, stood waiting for Koo to reveal his need.

Koo had labored a long time over his answer. Now he had it at the tip of his agile tongue. "We of the Macaque wish to leave this place that has been our home for so long. We, who have not had the gift of speech or of abstract thought for as long as your kind, wonder about the world outside the jungle. Before we leave a place we know well, will you tell us something of our destination?"

The Man sighed and sat on the ground beside the Macaque. "Will you go north? That is the direction taken by most who leave."

Koo dropped to hunker beside him. "We go north," he affirmed.

"Then I will tell you what we know...or have been told by those few who return from their journeying. Firstly, it is a very long way, and you can go as far as you wish. You may stop where you like, for very few of my kind now live in the

8

forests or on the plains of the lands north of our own."

Using a twig to make the lines, he drew a map on the ground. "There is the place Man used to call Mexico. Only along the coasts do people still live in towns, and they are very poor. Without the fish from the sea, they would starve. Above, here where the land widens out, is the place that was once called America. Forest covers it from the ocean, here, to the plains, which begin along this line. What lies west of that, we do not know, for no one has gone in that direction and returned to us."

Koo pointed to the ragged edge the Man had drawn. "And along the seacoast?"

"There are towns. A few. Each ruled by a petty ruler calling himself a King or herself a Queen. Or a Minister or a Potentate."

Koo glanced up at the huge parrot, which would have been capable, if so inclined, of carrying off either himself or the Man. "If you were moving northward, where would you go?" asked Koo.

"Up the coastline. You can find water where streams run into the sea. You can find Men who will trade food to you. You can fish, if need be. It will take a very long time for a group of Macaque to go. You will tire and stop. Your women will give birth and want to wait until the infants are larger. They will grow as you travel. It may take generations to reach your goal. Is it worth it to you?"

Koo fingered his medallion thoughtfully. He gazed at the wall of greenery that shut away everything beyond the small clearing. He thought of the wonderful things to see in those northern reaches where his kind had never gone. "It is worth it," he said. "Our thanks to you, friend. The word you bring will be valuable to us, as we make ready to go."

He watched the Man as long as he could see him on the path back to the river. His active imagination was turning the facts he had learned over and over. Would there be a place for his kind in that alien world?

He felt a sudden qualm. Would the Men there be wary of the Macaque, as even these had been for generations? Or would there be some skill, some task, some value that his people could provide to those in the distant north?

He could find no answer. He turned back toward the thicker jungle, where his people lived in huts high in the trees. Here they were safe to some extent. They understood the dangers and recognized them unerringly. There...there they would be like infants, ignorant of the perils they might encounter.

But they would go. Or if not, he would go alone. The jungle was too confined for his questing mind. He had had enough of the jungle.

CHAPTER ONE

It was a perfect day. Gem had known it would be when she saw the sun rise over the valley. Wild ducks had risen with the dawn from their marshy nests across the river, circling and quacking in the salt wind that blew seaward over the hills,

They could not quite see the ocean from their thatched cottage, which she shared with Big Nel and their son Little Nel. Even when she went high on the hills above the house and looked down to where their tiny valley lay in the curve of the river, she could not glimpse the waves. Now, busy gathering herbs for medicines and cooking, she moved among the trees on the slope above her home. She loved the days when there was an excuse to leave her household tasks to go into the woods and the hills. Even as she kept her eyes busy searching for the plants she needed she was enjoying the autumn-sweet air. It was a lovely day!

She had greeted her menfolk that morning with the whistled tune her mother had used when she herself was tiny. There were no words, but the tune itself was so cheerful that it brightened glum morning faces. Nel had circled her waist with his big arms, while their son had hugged her about the hips. They'd laughed together before she kissed them and slid away to set the meal on the table.

Then they had all gone about their day's work. Nel, testing the air for a hint of frost, decided to spend his day gathering the last of their vegetable crop from the plantings by the river's edge. If he began at once, he could secure them before the first frost. Little Nel, who found herb-gathering boring, elected to help his father.

"Bring your fishing pole," his father had suggested.

"Maybe you can catch a fish when you finish your part of the job."

Delighted, the boy had run for his equipment. In a few minutes the two were winding their way down the short path to the garden, the end of the pole making an exclamation point against the bright morning light on the river.

Left to herself, Gem had plaited her long auburn hair into twin braids. Then she fetched her wicker basket and her prod-stick. Moving happily along, she all but danced to the shed where the cows waited to be loosed into their hilly pasture.

"Gulla! Dewnose!" she greeted the beasts. "Eat well! Make fine calves for selling and good milk for drinking!" She opened the gate, letting them go free. They knew the morning ritual as well as she did.

Now, shading her amber eyes with her hand, she scanned the slope around her. She knew the land in their tiny valley as well as she knew Big Nel's face. Up on that ridge she would find rosemary. She herded the cows ahead of her for a time, until they turned aside to graze. The wind, cool and brisk, toyed with her skirt, which she held down as she forged ahead. A day like this made her feel good to be alive.

By midday, Gem had moved up the slope and down again. From time to time she had glanced down toward her laboring menfolk, who were almost just below her. She could see the even motions of Nel's hands as he gathered the crop. She could almost see the dip of Little Nel's bobber in the water as he concentrated on his fishing.

Her basket was almost full. Thyme and basil grew wild, with many medicinal herbs. She was a skilled healer. Not as good as her mother, perhaps, but the people of Dover Village called her when her mother was away or busy. Her mother...even Gem thought of her as Matron Bere. Lord Aubert himself called her by that title. But as respected as Bere was by those who knew her, she was revered most by her daughter, who knew her better than anyone.

Her basket was now heavy with leaves and roots. She found a soft patch of grass and sat down to rest. Around her the wind had scattered a carpet of multicolored leaves...soon the foliage would pass its peak of brightness. But all the land

12

still called New England would bask in radiance for a while before the cold time began.

Gem looked over the little valley. The farm was just below, and her two Nels were busy, still. The boy was sitting on the boulder, pole clutched in both hands. The fish line stretched taut along the current of the river. To her left was a dense copse, which became a wood of larger trees in the distance. Over the treetops a thin wisp of smoke curled into the sky. Was there a fire there? As she watched, the smoke thickened and grew blacker.

She stood up to peer at the enigmatic column. Several families lived in that direction. Yet the smoke seemed to be farther away.... Only the tiny military garrison on the estuary lay beyond. Could it have caught fire? Before she could decide, another column of smoke became visible. This was definitely nearer to her than the first. The farm of Clare and Ike? It was in the right direction.

A lump of apprehension began to form in her throat. What was happening out of her sight toward the sea? Something on the river caught her eye. A flash of brightness... water-shiny oars catching the sunlight?

Then she saw the longboat, its dark red sail the color of old blood, moving up the river. A golden bird flashed on the sail-cloth; even from such a distance it was clearly defined. Massive oars powered by strong muscles whipped the water, bringing the craft at an amazing clip toward the spot below her, where Nel and her son were unaware of their danger.

She shouted, "Nel! Hawkers! Beware!" but the morning breeze whipped her voice away, and those below could not hear her. She cursed the small cliff above the gardens; if she could go straight down, she could be there quickly, in time to warn them. But she had to go around by the path.

She forgot her basket and her poke-stick and began running as fast as she was able along the curving pathway. Even as she ran, she recalled everything she knew about the Seahawks. She had never seen them before, but the stories that were told made the skin goose pimple. There had to be at least forty men in that longboat. And Nel had never run from a fight in his life!

She ran harder, pounding along, ignoring the stitch in

her side, the tears streaming from her eyes. She knew that by now they were coming ashore, but she couldn't spare a glance. To fall now was to fail in her attempt to warn and help her family.

She heard, through the blood pounding in her ears, a furious shout. That was Nel. She knew that he was trying to fight off those men, and she sobbed with frustration. Now she was almost down the hill. Only the long stretch past the house and down to the river lay before her. The house stood between her and the river, and she rushed on, dreading what she would see when she rounded its bulk.

A shrill scream reached her ears. Little Nel!

"I'm coming, son!" she shouted, driving her numbing legs forward with all her strength. "Mother's coming!"

She rounded the house, but she couldn't see her husband or her son. She had no weapon. But she couldn't stop running toward the spot where they had been.

Two men dressed in leather, carrying axes, appeared from behind the house. They saw her and grinned, waving their axes. She tried to run faster, but her legs failed her at last. She had to stop, facing them, panting, trying to think what she might do to avoid them.

One man said something, but Gem couldn't understand his words. Her blood was thudding noisily in her, and her mind now seemed as numb as her legs. He moved toward her, dropping his axe. The other man joined him, and their dirty...and red-spattered...hands reached for her.

She found a last reserve of energy and tried to bolt. But it was too late.

A rough hand grabbed her wrist and twisted her about painfully, driving her face against a stinking chest. She tried frantically to push away, but a second paw took her throat and held on tightly. To struggle against that carefully applied pressure would strangle her.

She almost did that...and then she went quiet. To die now meant that she would never have revenge against the men who were disrupting her world. She had to survive to find what had happened to her husband and her son. No matter what, she had to remain alive.

They were ripping away her clothing. Her nakedness

seemed distant and unimportant. Even when they threw her to the ground and took turns at her, it seemed far away.

Not once did she cry out. When a series of terrible blows thudded into her limp body, she hardly knew, and when a last one struck her senseless, she went into the darkness gladly.

CHAPTER TWO

Randor, being the village hermit, cherished his privacy; when he heard the sounds of an approaching dog-rider, he cursed to himself. He had a beautiful deer hide curing on the back of his hut. He was ready to start making a warm winter jacket of the skin, and he didn't relish interruption.

As the panting of the dog drew nearer, however, he resigned himself to the inevitable and went around the hut to greet his uninvited company. The mount was a Dalmatian— he preferred German shepherds, himself, because of their fighting qualities, but Lord Aubert favored the showy spots of this breed. The animal had been ridden harder than was wise or normal. Saliva dripped from his lolling tongue, as his rider drew up in the yard.

"A toddler on his terrier knows better than to ride...," he had begun, when he saw that the rider was in worse state than his mount. The boy fell from the saddle. Randor, surprised, barely had time to catch him. Then he recognized the lad. The smith's elder son, Ranub. The boy was gasping, trying to catch his breath.

"Easy now," the old man said. He helped the boy to a bench against the wall. "Catch your breath. Then say what you've come to tell me."

The youth blinked, nodded. He drew several deep breaths, closed his eyes for a moment, and straightened against the wall.

"Sea...hawks! Coming!"

"What? Hawkers never come so far upriver. They raid the coast, with the safety of the sea behind them!"

The boy swallowed hard. "We thought that, too. That's why they were able to surprise the garrison. They were

16

throughour main gates before we knew they were near."

Randor had spent the better part of his life as a professional soldier, guarding the scanty human settlements from raiders and thieves. It was why he now liked being a hermit. He could imagine the bloody clash in that small stockade. Hawkers were notorious for savagery in combat. And the Lord's men would have been fighting for homes and families.

"Sergeant Lamon sent me after the Lord Governor for help. You must help me, Randor!"

Randor thought of the Queen's governor, Lord Aubert, located a hard ride to the west. It wasn't going to be in time, that aid.

"Easy, lad. Of course I'll help you. But you have to catch your wind and the dog must rest. What a shame all the horses died during the plague. They had more stamina for running while carrying weight, over a long haul. But that's in the past. It won't do any good at all if you and your mount collapse on your way. Come and lie a bit on my cot in the shade."

Slowly the graybeard helped the young messenger to his feet, steadying him carefully. The Dalmatian thrust her nose against Randor's chest. He patted her gently.

"Good dog! Come with us...we'll get you some water."

The mutated dog followed him to the well beneath a huge oak. After settling his charges in the shade, Randor drew fresh water and quenched the thirst of both, letting the dog drink her fill, at last, directly from the bucket.

The boy set aside his clay cup. "Look! Off yonder!" He pointed southward. Puffs of smoke rose above the tree-tops to tell a grim story.

"They're torching the homesteads along the river. Seaborn bastards!"

The boy rose unsteadily. "I can't stay. I must ride now to Lord Aubert."

Randor caught his arm. "Hold on. You'll be on your way soon enough. Sit and relax."

"But some of them might be coming this way!"

"I'm counting on that." Randor smiled coldly and went into his house. When he came out he was geared with all his old tools of war. About his tunic he had belted two scabbards. One contained a sword, the smaller holding a dirk at his left hip. Over his shoulder was a quiver filled with feathered shafts. Swinging from his right hand was a longbow. His reputation as a master bowman was still unequaled in the valley.

"I'm going into the woods to await our visitors. Stay here until you're properly rested, then take the track behind the hut, up the trout creek...you know the one?"

"Aye. My father and I used to fish along there."

"Good. When you reach the creek, there is a hunting track to the west."

The boy's eyes lit up. "It cuts through the hills!"

"It will save you hours of riding."

"Thank you, Randor." The boy looked sheepish. "I had forgotten that track."

"Men seldom have use for boyhood memories, more's the pity. Now rest. And tell Lord Aubert that old Randor will be conveying his greeting to any Hawkers coming this way."

Ranub took the old man's hand. "Good hunting, Randor!" The hermit turned to jog into the wood, and Ranub, watching him go, felt a twinge of pity for any pirates who might cross his path. Men like Randor did not grow too old to be dangerous enemies."

Once in the forest, Randor slowed his pace to a steady and comfortable gait that would carry him for hours without stress. He moved among the trees like the woodland creature he had become over the years. This was his natural habitat. His spirit was at peace here.

He traveled a deer trail that almost paralleled the main road from the river farms. As he moved, he kept glancing at the bright foliage toward that well-worn track. Coming at last to a clearing, he squatted in the thicket that an open glade and waited. Anyone crossing the clearing would make a perfect target. An ambush...simple, but the best and deadliest strategy, as one of his old commanders had told him, long ago.

Within an hour the theory was put to the test. A flutter of birds across the road warned him that someone was coming. Nocking an arrow, he came up on one knee to sight along the shaft. Three burly Seahawks emerged around a bend in the road at an easy lope. As they went across the clearing, laughing gutturally to themselves, Randor could see streaks of red glistening on their axes.

That was all he required. He loosed his first arrow. Using his soldier's skills, he aimed at the tallest man, who ran slightly behind the other two. As the arrow took him in the chest, his companions were still running ahead, unaware of anything wrong until he crashed to the ground behind them.

They turned and squatted beside the fallen man. The other, understanding at once that they had been attacked, spun to look around. As he squinted toward the tree line, the bow twanged a second time. The arrow caught him in the throat. He gave a startled cry, and his hands loosed the axe to clutch at the shaft protruding from his neck. Blood dripped through his fingers. He fell forward. The remaining man looked at him, then at Randor, who now stood in the road.

With a whoop, the big invader swung his axe aloft and charged toward the old man. Randor set a third arrow against the string. Sweat beaded his brow, as he brought the feathers to his cheek. There was no time for leisurely aim. The pirate loomed up before him, the axe swinging above his blond head.

When only yards separated them, the Seahawk flung his axe, but Randor's fingers had loosed the string an instant sooner. The man fell forward. As Randor relaxed, he felt the blade zip past his ear, touching his hair. Death had passed him by scant inches. Breathing hard, Randor saw that his last arrow had buried itself in the Hawker's gut, but somehow the fellow was struggling to his feet. They were tough birds to kill!

The wounded seaman came on, his hands pulling the knife at his belt. Randor scrambled backward, his old legs protesting. He danced edgewise as the pirate aimed a knife-blow at the spot where his head had been an instant before. Leaving his bow on the ground, the old man drew his own dirk and circled.

With another bellow, the scar-faced Hawker lunged again. This time Randor avoided his knife arm and thrust his steel into the other's heart with an expert blow. The Hawker stiffened, his body convulsing, then toppled at Randor's feet.

The old man spat into the dust. Then he kicked the life-less form, whose twitching was now merely dying nerves. As he retrieved the bow, Randor realized that the first victim was still moving, farther along the roadway.

"Bastards won't stay dead," he grumbled. He went to the gasping man, who lay on his back, holding the arrow that stuck up from his chest. Randor lost no time in slitting his throat.

Ignoring the weariness in his legs, he began dragging the bodies into the bushes, grumbling softly. He was definitely getting too old for this sort of thing.

* * * * * *

By the end of the day, Lord Aubert's men had arrived from the interior. They drove through the valley, seeking any marauders, but the Seahawks had already retreated to their boats and put out to sea. Helpless and unsuspecting victims were to their taste. Randor, with a few like him up and down the valley, had given them a taste of their own medicine, which they didn't relish at all.

As time went by, people began calling it the Autumn Raid. Once the differing stories of the survivors had been sorted out, the tale came clear.

Some sixty Seahawks had attacked the garrison in two long-boats. Once the forces in the fort had been quelled, most of them killed and the rest badly wounded, the Hawkers had split their forces and pressed inland to pillage wherever they could. In the process they laid waste to six farms, slaughtered fifty head of livestock, murdered ten of the valley-folk, and kidnapped eight children. Those, it was assumed, would be taken for sale in the slave markets in Portland. Among them was Gem's small son, Nel.

For all his ten years, Nel's life had been bounded by the river and the hills. Trips even to the village had been infrequent, but the boundless sky of his imagination had been filled by cloud-ships and dragons and many other shapes that his fancy wove. On either end of his universe, holding up that sky, had stood his father and mother. He couldn't imagine a world without either of them.

Now his father was gone. Nel had made it to the edge of the trees before his father had been killed. He might have run on to lose himself in the thickets, but something had made him turn to see how Big Nel fared. He had seen him die beneath the Hawker's axe.

Now Nel lay in the stinking bottom of the longboat, looking up with purest hatred at the feet and legs of the men rowing it downriver. They had killed his father. Probably his mother, too, for he knew she would have come as soon as she saw the attack. There was nobody who knew where he was. No one could be expected to try to rescue him. If it was done, he would have to do it himself. And he had no idea where he was being taken or what might be done with him.

He had no room for tears. What had happened was so hugely terrible that tears could give no relief. He lay in agony, radiating hatred in all directions. It was a wonder to him that the boots of the pirates were not scorched with it, that their leggings didn't burst into flame with the heat of his passion. But they didn't. Their owners rowed steadily on.

Before too long, he could tell by the pitching and rolling of the craft that they had reached the sea. Tied as he was and tossed carelessly among bales and boxes as if he were a thing instead of a person, he found himself rolling with that motion. The motion made him queasy. Bile rose in his throat. Behind him, he could hear someone being very sick. Surely that couldn't be one of the raiders.

He wriggled around, his sickness forgotten. A small boy, tied tightly, lay against a box, throwing up all over himself. The smell hit Nel as pure agony. His own stomach heaved, and his good breakfast spilled onto the deck.

When that was over, even sticky and nasty and miserable as he felt himself to be, he also felt better. His head seemed clearer. His mind was working again. He had been taught by both his parents to think carefully about problems, reason things out, step by step.

He needed a plan. He would escape. He would go home, even if the Hawkers had burned the cottage. He would go right on living where his parents had lived, proving their lives had not been wasted. For that to happen, he had to have

a plan. And, as well, a lot of good luck.
Thinking furiously, he fell asleep.

CHAPTER THREE

Cormal hated towns. He had spent his life, until now, in the woods. One who had survived the Long Hunt, a month in the forest as a boy, wresting from the forest all he needed, was not impressed by the things townsmen held dear.

On that hunt he had been responsible for his two cousins; the thought was still painful. An attack by thieves had costhim his kin and almost his life. Only his big strong body, his keen eyes, and his sharp wits had brought him, living, from that encounter. He knew three names...those of the attackers still living. Nadak, Ferros, and Durnam still walked the world, and one day he would find them.

Now, as he sat on the doorstone of the inn from which he had just been forcibly ejected, he was recalling his thirty *years in* the woods, where he had grown to prefer the animals to man. His panther-tawny hair ruffled in the wind from the sea, and his panther-brown eyes stared past the filth of the street toward the clean sky over the ocean.

What was he doing here? He had made the long journey to the big lakes, which spread from horizon to horizon, beyond the forest to the west. He supposed that the sight of those lakes was what made him want to see even bigger waters, once he learned that an ocean lay to the east. And now he was here. But the cleanness of the waves was polluted by the slops that were poured into the streets, as well as by the ugly natures of many of the shore's inhabitants.

He loved the crashing of the rough waves onto the stones of the shore...that spoke to something deep inside him. But he had made a fool's errand, nevertheless. He had found no sign of his enemies here. And the people were flea-infested, self-satisfied, and unwashed. Not one was as wor-

23

thy, he thought, as any bearfox in the woods.

He hunted in the near forests and sold game for drinking money. The innkeepers, being typical Portlanders, wanted his hard-won meat for as nearly nothing as possible, and when the last one bargained too far, he had bent the man's ears into interesting shapes. That was why he now sat outside, instead of inside, this particular inn, watching the breeze ripple the puddles of muddy water.

As he mused, his eyes fell on the strangest little man he had ever encountered in his life, and his grin faded away. Muffled in a cloak, for it was early winter though snowless as yet, the object of his attention walked very awkwardly. The feet beneath his cloak were swaddled in ungainly moccasins and looked entirely too wide for human feet.

Others had noticed the little fellow, too. A gang of small boys pelted toward him, rocks in their hands, wickedness in their eyes. Cormal let the small man pass him. Then he rose to his full height and stepped in front of the leader of the boys. He didn't have to say a word. The thin-faced lad blinked and dropped his rock. Then he and his bunch slunk away into an alley.

Cormal took up his pack and followed the small figure as it picked its way among the slops of the street. "Ho, friend!" he called, as the little man paused before the coffee house. "Would you bear me company in a bit of food and a cup of something hot on this dismal day?"

The figure turned, and Cormal almost dropped his pack. The face within the hood was merry, with bright eyes that twinkled with intelligence. But it wasn't a human face. There was a resemblance, true, but the mouth was wide, more of a muzzle than a nose. And it was covered with fur, except for the area about the eyes and mouth, where pinkish-brown skin showed.

"Wit ples're," it said. Its accent was even stranger than its appearance. "I was think, just now, s'bad to eat alone."

Stunned, but game for anything, Cormal pushed open a door and stepped into the steamy interior of the coffee house. He wondered what coffee had really been, back when that name had been given to a hot drink. No such thing existed now, he was sure. They served mint teas, brewed ales, barley that had been toasted and ground and boiled. Stronger things, too, of course, but Cormal's weak head for such drink led him to steer clear of those.

He found a table and slung his pack beneath it. He gestured for his companion to sit opposite him. When the fellow's cloak slid back over the chair, it was obvious that this person had never been a human being. It was not Cormal's way to mince words.

"What are you?" he asked bluntly.

A chitter of laughter rose from the wide mouth. "You never h'rd of Macaque? Fr'm south. V'ry far."

Cormal stared. He had heard of Macaque, sure, but he had no idea that the reality would be so strange.

"The monkey-men who came up from the hot country after the plague...I'd thought they must be some one's flight of fancy," he reminded himself softly. "It's a pleasure to meet one of your kind."

The creature's gaze was sharp as he studied the man across the table. Then he said, "You eat? I buy!"

That was to Cormal's liking. His pouch, never bulky, was now pretty flat, what with the stinginess of the shopkeepers and the high price of everything from food to lodging. He looked up to see a husky girl, hand on hip, waiting for his order.

"Something hot...barley, I think. You have soup today?"

"Stew. Freshly made, with mutton and venison."

"That will do. And bread, if you've any made of grain milled fine. I can't abide the gravels in most of the bread here." He looked over at the Macaque.

That worthy chittered again with amusement. Then he gave his order, and they were left to gaze at each other.

"You not angry, see not-man in street? In eat-place?" the creature asked.

"Why? I'm used to seeing bears in the woods, and they don't make me angry. Or eagles in the sky, or fish in the river. And some of the things I've seen in these streets make you seem like a breath of sanity. Besides, they tell me your kind has useful gifts. Can you truly tell when the Seahawks are coming?"

Sadness filled the dark eyes. "Can do. Send ahead much

25

hate, much fear. We feel. We know. See, sometime, feel always. Bad. Dangerous. Come here under truce-flag, now. Sell slave." The eyes looked into Cormal's, and there was a question in them. "You like slave?"

Cormal spat into the sawdust of the floor. "Cannot abide the thought. No self-respecting creature would be one or buy one. Makes me want to pick up something and knock off some heads."

The Macaque's sigh sounded very human. "We, too. Slave bad thing. Seahawk bad thing. Two t'geth'r, v'ry bad thing. Come tomorrow, both t'geth'r. You stay to see?"

Cormal didn't reply until his bowl of stew was set before him and the girl had gone. Then he stared at the little person. He seemed to want something...some commitment.

"I might. Don't like the town. Don't like the people. But I do like to see new things."

A skinny, black-furred hand snaked across the table to take his in a surprisingly strong grip. "Name Koola. Come t'morr'w. Here. I meet. We go to slave-place t'geth'r?"

"I will," said Cormal "but I'd like to know why."

The small person looked down at his bowl of vegetables. When his gaze again met Cormal's, the eyes were thoughtful. "S'mbody come. V'ry full of hate. Not 'fraid like most slave. We see who, why, t'morr'w."

* * * * * * *

The next day was even more dismal than its predecessor. The wind whipsawed from northeast to north. There was an edge of deadly chill to it. When Cormal met Koola at the coffee house, they both had something hot to drink before daring the morning.

The slave pens, when they found them, were filthy. The longboat must have come into harbor in the night, for there were eight small children, six men, and four women those draughty spaces.

"Empty b'fore," said Koola shortly.

All the children were together in one pen. They were spent with crying, dirty and cold and miserable.

Big blond men stood about, watching their livestock,

26

urging would-be buyers to take a closer look. Cormal stepped warily about them, hating the stink of their leathers, the look of their cold blue eyes. His gut felt greasy and sick when he looked at the slaves. Then his eye was caught by one who wasn't huddled into the mass of unhappy flesh, trying to warm himself. He sat apart, his skin bluish with cold, his back straight. When Cormal's gaze met the boy's, he flinched at the hatred that blazed out.

Blond hair, tousled and full of debris, hung about a thin face. The child was pale, but Cormal felt that it was anger, not fear, that had drained all the color from his face.

The big man looked down at the Macaque. "That's the one." It was not a question.

The small creature nodded.

Cormal caught the eye of one of the Hawkers. "That one," he said, pointing.

The man spat into the mud. "That one's not for sale. Rest of 'em are trash, good for nothing but hard work. That 'un's got the making of a Hawk in 'im. We're going to keep 'im."

The Macaque tugged at Cormal's cloak. The big man dipped his dark head to hear. "Sev'nty gilds I got. You?"

Cormal felt his pouch. "Ten argents. We'll see." That amount would be more than a fair price for the boy, if the haggling going on around them was a sign. Cormal felt that there was a chance that good gold and silver might change the Hawkers' minds. But it didn't. The seamen sold out their other stock before noon to the large landholders who'd made the long trek from down the coast or had come up all the way from York State to find strong backs for their fields. The Hawkers spent some time in the lowest of the drinking houses, then sailed away into the afternoon, taking the boy with them.

Cormal looked across the darkening waters after the sail. He knew he would be haunted by those blue eyes for a long time...perhaps forever.

Koola sighed. Cormal touched his head. Neither of them would forget.

CHAPTER FOUR

Gem had come back from darkness into a shattered world with a body so bruised and torn that it was weeks before she could walk. Despite her mother's most intensive care, she cried out in the night, rousing from nightmares that left her shaking and sick. And even awake, she lay for long hours, holding down the tears that threatened to spill every time she thought of her lost men.

Nel...gone, battered to death, stabbed, slashed by his attackers so that those who buried him refused to describe his body to her. And small Nel, who was now adrift someplace with the beasts that had killed his father...the thought tortured her.

When at last Gem could again bear to move, to exercise, and finally to walk haltingly about the village, she knew that her life was changed past anything she could have dreamed in her worst moments. She knew, too, that something waited to be done. Once she had healed enough to think clearly, what it was would become apparent to her.

Finally, after more weeks, she was able to walk the distance to her cottage, and she limped the long way, thinking about what had happened to her and the task she had to do. The bones of the cottage thrust up through the burned timbers like those of a dead animal, she thought, as she stood beside the ruined cowshed. The cows now were stabled with a neighbor, and even their scent was gone from their former home.

Gem drew a deep breath to quell the queasiness in her stomach. The wound inside her heart was not healed...would never heal, she began to think, though her mother had talked gently with her, and the elders had come also, trying to help

28

her with her terrible loss. Even as they tried to comfort her, she felt in them the pain of their own losses, for few were the families in Dover that had not lost at least one member in this autumn raid.

Pain, however, was a part of life. Gem could deal with that. She was a healer, after all, like her mother. The wounds in her soul were unfamiliar, however. For all her control, her agony sometimes twisted inside her in the midst of the most everyday occupation. And at night—never before had she been wakened from devastating dreams by her own screams.

Through it all, her mother had watched with pain almost the equal of her own. Now she felt ashamed of the time Matron Bere had given to her, while also caring for all those wounded from the garrison and the outlying areas.

"Poor Mother," she said softly. "I might have helped you, instead of sniveling like a child."

Yet Matron Bere had been more than equal to her tasks. She had organized the village people, made a hospital of the town meeting-hall. Supervising. Advising, scolding, managing, she had kept those alive who had a chance and eased the deaths of those who had not. When Lord Aubert came riding into Dover on his coal-black Dalmatian, he had come to thank her personally.

Matron Bere had been flabbergasted when the Lord bent over her hand and kissed it. Gem recalled her expression with amusement, even though she knew that the honor had been more than well deserved.

"Gem!"

She turned, stirring up a small cloud of soot from her cottage. Matron Bere herself was moving down the path, her staff tapping the earth as she came. As she drew near, she realized once again how much alike she and her mother were in appearance. They even possessed identical dispositions. And tempers. Gem saw evidence of her mother's displeasure written plainly on her face.

"What are you doing here?" asked Matron Bere.

"I had to come. Don't be angry, Mother."

"Don't tell me not to be angry when I have good cause! Do you hear me?"

"I'd be deaf if I didn't. Please don't shout!" Gem knew

29

her tone was acid, but disagreements with her mother did things to her that she couldn't explain.

"Don't shout!" Matron Bere's face was growing redder by the moment. She faced Gem squarely, but the girl didn't flinchfrom her steely gaze. At last Matron Bere thumped her stick into the ashes and shook her head in resignation.

"And what am I to do with you, girl? You should, damn it, still be abed. You know that very well. I've taught you too well for you not to."

Moved by an impulse, Gem stepped closer and hugged her mother. Choking back the betraying tears, she said, "Mother, it still hurts so very badly!"

The matron dropped her cane in the ashes and put her arms about her daughter, stroking her hair as she had done when Gem was a child.

"I know it, love. Oh. I know it. When your Pa went, all those years ago, I learned that terrible emptiness of the heart. A cold and miserable thing. But I survived it, and so will you."

Gem, sniffing, stepped back to stare at her mother. She did understand. As long as Matron Bere lived, Gem would never be entirely alone. Yet there was a great void in the middle of what had been her self. An emptiness surrounding her wreckage. "I feel so empty! How did you stop it from hurting?" she asked.

"I didn't, love. Time did. It will for you. Believe it— cling to that belief, and you will see. Days will smooth your memories as they pass. Then only the good will be left to you. Give it time."

Crows skittered across the sky. A gust of wind rustled the grass. Gem bent to retrieve her mother's staff, and together they made their way out of the sooty rubble.

"You should not have come here," Matron Bere said.

"Something drew me. I wanted to see Nel's grave."

"It's down by the water. Lord Aubert told me his men attended to it. They were all Nel's comrades, when he served in the militia. He was a good man, Nel. He made good friends."

Gem rubbed her hands across her eyes. She was sick of crying. Sick of feeling weak and ill and frightened. She was made of stronger stuff than that.

"Yes, he was. I would mourn him properly for a year, a month, a week and a day...if I didn't have other things do."

"Other things?" Matron Bere looked puzzled.

"I must find little Nel." Gem stared into her mother's eyes.

Matron Bere took her arm and shook it. "That is madness. Nothing less than madness."

"He is my son. Nel's son."

"I know that. But do you think that you are the only woman to lose a child to the Seahawks? Or a husband, for that matter? Do you think that you, of all women, can accomplish a thing that all the men cannot?

"He is gone! If little Nel wasn't sold as a slave in Portland by now, he is a prisoner on one of the hundred islands Seahawkers rule. No one has ever survived to tell of Hawker captivity, Gem. It would be better to think of him dead."

Gem pulled her arm free. She had known that this would be the reaction, not only of her mother but of everyone else.

"I will not forget my son and just continue with my life. Is that what all those others do? Is that the normal way? Well, it is not mine."

"What else can you do?"

"I can find him and bring him home."

"Impossible! A woman...a farmer's wife! What do you know of the world beyond this valley? Or of the warlike skills needed to survive out there in the wild lands?"

"Nothing...but I intend to learn." Gem stood her ground beneath her mother's shocked gaze.

"And how will you manage that?"

"I will go to Randor. He can teach me. He can tell me about the world outside our valley. Then I will go and find Nel."

Matron Bere raised her hands in frustration. "Foolish girl! Randor is a sour old man, loving solitude more than anything else. What makes you think he will consent to teach a foolish girl?"

Gem didn't budge. "If he will not, then another will. Somewhere, I will find someone who will teach me skill at arms which I must know. But Randor will be the first one I ask. He is the best there is. Then, when I have learned, I will find and rescue my child." She stared out over the river, for they had come almost to its edge.

"Mother, don't you see that I can do nothing else? If I do nothing, if I let Nel remain lost, then I cannot live. My mind is made up,"

Matron Bere had lived more than half a century. She had seen the doings of men and women, the twistings of fate and circumstance. She had learned to live with the things she couldn't change.

She touched her daughter's cheek. Her voice was soft when she said, "Yes. I can see that. Nothing I say will change you, no matter what dangers you face or how far you must go. But you will take my heart with you."

Gem made no answer, but she clasped her mother's hand. They were approaching the mound that was Nel's grave. The soldiers had put Nel beneath the wide-spread branches of the first big oak. Its canopy covered the pile of stones with a peaceful shadow. Gem bent to gather wild ferns from the forest edge.

She laid the ferns atop the cairn and looked down at dappling of light and shade. Already a fine mist of moss was forming on the stones. She quietly let slip the remnants of her past life. These memories now served only to weaken her resolve. Nel was gone into the hereafter, but their son still lived. She must focus her life upon that thought alone.

She turned from the grave and took her mother's hand Together they turned their backs on that peaceful spot and left it behind them.

* * * * * * *

It was late afternoon. The clearing where Randor had his hut was already lapped in evening shadow when Gem came through the trees. She stopped to gaze at the soldierly arrangement of the house and shed and work-benches.

Matron Bere had told her to be polite but firm. Though she had heard tales of Randor for most of her life, Gem had never seen the old soldier. Now she was about to interrupt him as he sat at a bench, near his front door. He appeared to be lost in his task of waxing a new bowstring made of catgut. She suddenly felt doubtful about her careful scheme. Her step slowed. Then she thought of her son and moved forward boldly, her heart thudding against her ribs.

Randor had seen the girl as soon as she reached the edge of the trees. He made no sign, however. He was annoyed at the intrusion. Since he had killed those raiding Hawkers, the village people had thought it necessary to treat him as some sort of hero. All Lord Aubert's doing, for praising a simple act of soldiering.

People had been popping up ever since, carrying gifts to show their gratitude. He had eaten more vegetables than he liked to think of. One earnest soul tried to give his cow, and only his insistence that milk made him ill had kept him from being burdened with the beast.

If he'd been a farmer, he never could have taken care of those Hawkers so easily. No. He was a hunter, and before that a soldier. Those in Dover would have been astonished now at what a well-known soldier he had been, in the old days when he had served from one end of the known lands to the other. The name of Randor was still, he suspected, held up to new recruits in distant places as an example of soldiery at its best.

He had been civil to the farmers, he hoped. They couldn't help being what they were. He had liked the spice cakes and the wine and the quilt the cobbler's wife had made for him. He didn't admit it...hardly did even to himself...but he'd enjoyed those things.

Now he wound the tough string around the wooden nails in his bench and wondered what gift this newcomer might bring. Then he noted that she was empty-handed. Even stranger than that was the way she was dressed.

She wore a belted tunic, below which were trousers and fine walking boots reaching to mid-calf. Her hair was in two braids, but that was the only thing about her that seemed properly female. In addition to her costume, she possessed an air of determination that he found oddly disturbing. He found himself studying her face as she opened her mouth.

"Greeting, Master Randor."

He put down his bowl of wax and frowned at her. A

clean, open face, he thought. Honest eyes, filled with pain. He needed no more pain!

"No masters here, girl. Name is Randor!" he growled.

"We respect you. I meant no harm," she said.

"No offense taken," he grunted. "Who might you be?"

"Gem. My mother is Matron Bere."

"Aha!" Randor knew the name, if no other in the village. "What brings her daughter to old Randor? I am a busy man and fond of my own company."

She blushed under his gaze. "Forgive me. I've come to ask your help. I need...I need to learn weapons and the skills for using them. The sword, the bow, and the knife."

He blinked. Only by that did he betray his astonishment. "The way of the blade is hard, even for men."

She straightened. He could see the fine play of muscle along her shoulders under the tight-fitting tunic. Her gaze was as direct as his own.

"Seahawks took my only son, killed my man. I will go after them to bring my child home again. No one else will do it. And I must be able."

Randor ran his hand across the gray brush of his beard as he studied her. There was no bravado in her words or her tone. A wild scheme, but a matter-of-fact attitude, he thought.

"And why should I teach you? What can you give in payment for the lessoning?"

"I have no money. But I will be your servant. I will cook and clean for you all the time you teach me."

Randor snorted. "Clean! That is the last thing I want, young woman. Cookery is a thing I do my own way, too. Had I wanted a servant I could have chosen from the best house-dames of the village, after the raid. I need no such service. It would waste my time to teach you." He looked down at his work, but from the corner of his eye he studied her expression.

She bit her lip. Her fists clenched, but she made them relax as she said, "Then forgive me for wasting your time. You are the best warrior I know. I want to learn only from the best, for I will need such skills where I must go. But there will be someone, somewhere, who will teach me, even if they are not the equals of Randor."

She turned to go, but his voice stopped her. "And do you really think flattery will win over a man like me?"

Gem spun about, anger flushing her cheeks. "Think what you will, old man. I want my son. I will have him. I came to Randor the Hermit because I have heard, all my life, about your skill, your courage, and your honesty. Perhaps I was wrong to believe such village gossip."

"What?" He looked shocked.

"I think I spoke clearly. I thought they were the tales the old tell to impress the young. But the affair of the Seahawks was another thing. It was here and now. My man's blood was just freshly spilled when you took revenge for him. I came here for help because I thought you to be the only one who might understand my need for action...for justice, if you will. Having seen your scarred face and your hands, I now believe all those tales I doubted before. It speaks from your voice and your stance. You are without a doubt the greatest soldier ever to live in the valley. That is obvious, even as it is also obvious that your ego is as big as your skill. Good day, old man."

Randor twisted his knees free of the bench and rose. "Hold on, now, and don't be getting your neck-hair up. Come here, girl."

She stepped toward him, staring into his face. Then she put her tough little hands into his big paws. He took them and looked them over carefully. She was a bit taller than he, and he had to twist his neck to look up into her face.

"I have taught women before this, in years gone by." A gleam touched his eyes for an instant; then it was gone. Again he was all business. Now he was revealing a snaggle-toothed grin. "You have spirit, girl. I like that."

She sighed. "I will work very hard to learn."

"By gadfry, you'll have to, Gem of Dover. I'm old, as you point out, and it's likely that you'll be my last pupil. I've outlived my time by quite a bit, already."

She realized that this was the acceptance she had wanted...and dreaded. She was undertaking a monumental task that would alter her life.

Now he was frowning, but it was not ill temper that

shone in his eyes. "I'll teach you to overcome your lack of size and reach. To use what weight you've got in the most effective ways. We'll work until you will want to use the blade on me, instead of your enemies. But we'll not stop until you've reached the very top of what you can become."

He looked away into the darkness as he added, "You'll be the last, but the best. You hear that? You'll be the best of 'em all!"

CHAPTER FIVE

While he was in the slave pens of Portland, Nel saw, in a dream, a Macaque trying to buy him from his captors. On the voyage Nel thought often about the monkey-man, and he listened to the Hawkers' wild tales about the abilities of such creatures to sense their approach and to warn intended victims of lightning raids.

Nel wished the little being had bought him. He would rather learn to be a monkey than to be a pirate. Then the voyage ended....

Nel would never forget his first glimpse of Blood Island. The Hawkers had talked about their safe haven during the long trip from Portland, and even in his shocked state of mind the boy had taken note of the things they said.

His first day on the island was a sign of things to come. The ship had anchored at a dock that was also a small fortress. Above it was a collection of stone houses. He was dragged ashore beneath the forbidding walls and tied to a post on the wharf while his captors unloaded the booty they had kept for their own use.

Slatternly women and grimy children clamored about the pier, welcoming relatives and friends. Nel thought at first they were much like the people he had left behind at Dover. Soon, however, he saw how rough and cruel they were, as well as how obviously they lacked the discipline and the ordered ways of thinking he had known all his life. Even the men unloading the ship worked in a slipshod manner that wasted time and caused chaos on the dock and would have been funny, if he had felt like laughing.

Most of the people ignored him. A few children stared at him, their mouths hanging half open as if they were lackwits.

Among them was a gangling girl with stringy brown hair, who looked him over with round silver eyes, her expression disdainful. At last she spat a curse, her thin lips curling contemptuously. "Dirt-grubber," she sneered.

Though his hands were tied, Nel had the use of his feet. He kicked out lustily, catching her on the shin. The smack of heel on bone cracked through the air, and the girl seemed to go into a frenzy. She dived at him, nails tearing at his skin. Only a passing pirate, who hauled her off the bound boy, saved him from losing his eyes to her attack.

The man caught her roughly by the scruff of the neck and shook her. "Dida! Don't spoil the prize catch afore your Pa gets a look at him. This 'un will be a Hawk, by and by. You blind him, he's good for nothing but fish bait."

She sneered, "A dung-wader? Don't make me laugh, Tarl. He be only a dirt-grubber, good for nothing useful at all. Let me go, or I'll see that Jacker gets after you."

The pirate laughed and booted her thin flanks to send her on her way. She paused at the end of the wharf, rubbing her backside. Nel was astonished at the look of hatred she sent his way. He hadn't done anything to her!

He gritted his teeth, wishing he could strike them all dead with lightning and thunder. They didn't deserve to live! His father was slain, the cottage set afire. He didn't know what had happened to his mother, and he tried not to think about that. In that moment, he determined to destroy their world as thoroughly as they had his. He made a vow, and it was one he intended to keep.

Once the Hawkers had their loot within the walls, they took their captive and made their way to the plaza inside the fortress. The pirate named Tarl, who seemed to be in charge, tied the boy's hands together with a length of rope and tugged him after him as if he were a pet goat.

Tarl greeted a few others, who seemed to be captains, and they all went together into the large hall facing the plaza. The hall was long and wide and filled with tables, at which many pirates were drinking and eating in the most repulsive manner the boy had ever seen. His captors paid no heed to the revelers but marched Nel into the center of the room and stood him up before a raised platform.

In the light of the braziers Nel could see three men sitting at a special table. Big men. The one in the center was biggest of all, with massive shoulders and meaty arms ending in fists like hams. Eyes surrounded by a curling mop of hair and an equally curly beard, stared at him.

"Ho!" boomed a deep voice. "Welcome to port, Captains. Thom, Tarl, Opul: was the hunting good this season?"

The captains hastened to give reports on their coastal raids, interrupting each other and flourishing their arms as they spoke. Nel, listening to them, relived the cowardly attack on his unarmed father. As horror mounted on horror, told as prideful accomplishment instead of ugly acts of evil, he was sickened at their savagery.

When the report was completed, the crowd cheered. Tankards were thumped on dirty tables, and the listeners stamped their heavy feet with approval.

The big chief of them all ran his fingers through his fiery beard. "Well done, men. You've done us proud. We're well found for the winter, now the new stocks are in the sheds. But what have you there at the end of your tether, Tarl? A different sort of fish, eh?"

Tarl pulled Nel forward until he was directly opposite the man at the table. The boy glared up at the pirate chief, forcing himself not to flinch as those red-rimmed eyes met own.

"Cap'n Jack, this be one grubber with the grit most lack. His old man fought us with a hoe, too, so there's fighting blood in him. We had to kill the old 'un, when he offed Juniper with the handle of that hoe. When Crack Johns split the man's head, the boy jumped him with only his fists. Johns still has black spots on his dirty hide from those little bits of hands. The boy never showed yellow, never whimpered nor whined. We wouldn't sell him, thinking you might like to make a Hawker out of him."

Jacker looked down thoughtfully. "We're always short of hands. What say you, boy?"

Nel glared at him, lips folded thin. He didn't reply.

"Speak up! When I ask, men answer."

Tarl cuffed the boy behind the ear and growled, "When Cap'n Jacker speaks, boy, you talk up smart-like. You hear me?"

Off-balance, Nel stumbled a half-step forward. He straightened at once and stared up at the captain, defiant and alone. "I'm not afraid of you," he said. "You're cowards and murderers. Go ahead...kill me. You don't scare me a bit!"

Captain Jacker flung back his flaming head and guffawed. He slapped his chest with a huge hand, and when he had himself under control again he said, "Well spoke, lad. So we don' scare you a bit, eh?"

"No." Nel bit out the word and stood silent, seething with anger.

Suddenly Jacker's right hand flickered with a motion too swift to follow. A dirk seemed to dart from sleeve to palm to flight so quickly that only a flash of reflected light showed its path. The blade thunked into the boards between Nel's feet.

The boy gave an involuntary jerk. Then he forced himself to stand still. Had the pirate meant to miss him? Probably, he thought. Such expert use of the blade didn't hint at misses when hits were intended. Fury ran along his veins like fire. He bent and jerked the knife free. In the same motion, he leaped onto the dais. Holding the blade in both hands, he set the point toward the giant on the other side of the table. Bracing it between both hands, he lunged head-first at Jacker.

Tarl grabbed him by the end of his tunic before he reached his goal. He pulled him backward off the board and stood him upright beside him, snatching the dirk from his hands in the process.

Jacker was roaring with laughter. His lieutenants were laughing, too, and the entire hall joined in. Tarl lifted his hand to hit the boy, but Jack waved him off. "Let him be. What's your name, Fire-eater?"

Nel looked straight into those bloodshot eyes. "Little Nel," he said, his voice oddly choked and gruff.

"You're no 'little' anything, lad. One who comes after Captain Jack with his own dirk is big enough for most things. Nel's your name, eh? It's what you'll be called. Tarl, give me the blade. I'll cut off the ropes."

A hand the size of a small boulder came forward and set

the haft of the dirk into it. Nel saw the exchange with some apprehension. Surely the man couldn't mean what he had said? But Jacker came around the table, caught the boy's bound hands in one of his own beefy paws, and severed the rope neatly. Nel stepped back, rubbing numbed wrists. He was bewildered. Why did this man he hated so bitterly cut him free?

The Hawker tousled the boy's fair hair, grinning down at him. "We need men with fire. Now ye be one of us. You've the makings of a real Hawk, too. This'll be your home."

"No! Dover is my home!"

A sharp voice came from the corner of the room. "Listen to the mud-grubber, Pa!"

The skinny girl stepped from behind a table and walked arrogantly to stand beside her father. She was still grimy, her lank hair straggling down her back.

The captain watched her with amusement. "Why say you so, Daughter?"

Nel's heart thudded into his boots. Of all the people on the island, he would have to kick the shins of the captain's daughter.

"He's nothing but a farmer...you can see it all over him. He hates us, too. Cut him into bits and feed him to the gulls!" she sneered.

The red eyebrows drew down above the keen eyes. "Now what be chewing on you, Dida?" Jacker asked.

Tarl spoke from behind Nel. "She set in to bullyraggin' him, down on the pier. While he was tied to a post."

"Oh? And then what?"

"We'd tied him proper to the wharf post. Dida gave him a bit of her ladylike chit-chat. Then she spit at him, and he give 'er a good 'un on the knee bone. She went wild, seems like. Had to drag 'er off him, or she'd of tore his eyes out."

The Captain looked down at his untidy offspring. He didn't look happy. "Serves you right, girl. I've told you more than once to put a reef in that temper of yours. Look to it, 'fore I take a hand."

She didn't cringe, but Nel saw something shrink inside her. Probably at the thought of what those ham-like hands

41

could do.

"I was only funnin', Pa."

Jacker frowned. "I know all too well the kind of funnin' that you do. We'll talk about that later. Now I tell you straight—leave this 'un alone. And get yourself home before I bare your tail and whale you proper."

Her cheeks reddened. She stalked away stiffly, choosing to walk around the table in order to pass Nel. When she reached his side, she paused long enough to breathe, "I'll get you, Grubber!" Then she ran from the hall.

Jacker stared after her for a moment. Then he shook his head as if to clear it of something unpleasant. "Bolton One-Leg!" he boomed.

From a couple of tables down came a cracked reply, "Aye, Sir."

A wiry fellow, shaved bald as an egg, rose from his seat and hobbled toward the dais. When he got clear of the tables, Nel could see that he stumped along on one leg. The other ended at the knee, where it met a chunk of wood whittled to a tapered tip cased in metal. He made a distinctive clacking as he crossed the stained boards of the floor.

When he stopped before the platform, Jacker said, "Bolton. I charge you with Nel. Take him home and teach him the ways of the Hawks, with the other boys."

The man grinned, his snaggled teeth dark in his weathered face. "Aye, Cap'n. Happy to. He's got the stuff, seems certain. Come, boy, let's go."

Nel looked at him, then at Jacker. Things were moving so fast that he hardly knew how to react.

"Go with him, Nel," the captain commanded. "One-leg is as fine a Hawk as any you'll find. Go with him and do what he says. That's my orders. You'll find that my order is the only thing that matters on Blood Island. This is not Dover."

Nel stepped off the dais and followed his new warden out of the hall. He knew that he didn't want to be a Seahawk, no matter how great an honor it might seem to that crew In the eating hall. Yet he was intelligent enough be realistic. He had no choice. Not now....

For the time being he would do what he had to in order

to survive. He would have his revenge. If it took pretending to be one of them for now, then so be it. He would become a Seahawk, in order to use their own skills against them.

* * * * * * *

That was not so easily done. The boy doubted his ability to survive the training. Every morning, come sun or storm, the boys were taken into the freezing waters in three small skiffs. Several older Hawks, too infirm for active duty, were in charge of their training. A couple of miles out, they stripped and were heaved overboard, to swim ashore.

The first time, Nel thought he couldn't possibly live through the ordeal. When the icy waters of the Atlantic closed over his head, he had gasped, but he hadn't screamed, as a few of the boys did. He kicked out with numbed legs and surfaced.

Around him other boys were popping to the tops of the waves, treading water as the big swells threatened to swamp them. Nel didn't wait. He pulled in a lungful of cold air and turned his back on the bobbing longboat, heading for the island as fast as his freezing limbs could propel him.

He blessed his father for teaching him to swim when he was tiny. If he hadn't been an accomplished swimmer, he would have gone to the bottom—and even as the thought passed through his mind, he heard behind him a despairing gasp. A shrill voice shrieked, then was cut off suddenly.

He turned to look behind. The dark head that had been right behind him was gone. Nel shook the wet hair from his eyes and stared hard, but the water was gray-pale and impenetrable. He wanted to dive for his lost companion, unknown though he might be, but he knew his limits, knew it would mean his own death.

The boy turned again toward Blood Island and swam frantically, feeling the blood warm in his veins, even as the water chilled his skin. The island beckoned him, and he kept his mind focused on that. Nothing but that.

That was only the first of many long swims. Every morning the same drill...and many times they counted fewer boys at the end of it than they had done at the beginning. He

43

hardened with the harsh training. Three miles in a cold rough sea every morning strengthened him unbelievably.

Often Nel looked up as he came ashore to see Dida watching from a cliff top. Rubbing himself down with a rough blanket, he would think of his determined enemy. She watched him constantly. She would make trouble for him, if she could.

After the swim, the boys were made to run along the beach, the full circumference of the island. The pace left them wobbly legged and out of breath when they reached the docks at last. A breakfast of goat milk, gravelly bread, and rank cheese would have turned Nel's stomach before. The exertion and his hunger made it almost delicious.

That proved to be only the beginning of the day for the buys. Then came work. Nel had been no stranger to net-mending and net-making and boat-scraping. He had done such work with his father along the river. But that seemed more like play as he looked back on it. No matter how fast his hands were with the shuttle, knotting the nets, a rope's end always waited to make him move more quickly yet.

Afternoons were given over to weapon-handling. Bolton was the instructor. Nel found that the one-legged man, a master of knife and double-edged sea-axe, was held in awe by all the boys because of his skill and courage as a fighter.

Billy, the only plump boy on the Island, told exciting tales of the old man's prowess as a pirate. While waiting their turns, Billy shared some of those gruesome stories.

"When Cap'n Jack took over Blood Island, Bolton was one of his captains. Together they mustered twenty good crews to challenge old Dan'l Tooth."

"Who's Dan'l Tooth?" Nel asked.

"You never heard of old Toother? He was the fiercest pirate ever. He found this island and commenced to build it up. He didn't want to share it with others, either. Wanted to keep the safe harbor and hidden anchorage for hisself alone, and his crews. Jack wanted to bring all the Hawkers together, under one command. Wanted to base 'em here where they'd be safe in the off-season. Toother hated the notion. See?"

Nel nodded, fascinated.

"One summer day, right out yonder beyond the head-

44

land, they met. Toother and all his crews were cocked and primed. Cap'n Jack was the same. Tooth had thirty ships and Jack had twenty, but if Toother had the edge in the ships, Jack did in crews. They were the best, and the meanest, to be found. I know...my Pa was one of 'em. He was there, and he saw it all."

Nel could see in his mind the fleets squaring off in the waters beyond the headland. "Then what?" he asked.

"Jack took the lead, looking for Tooth in the flagship. When he found him, he cut off his head with one swipe of his blade, so they say. But a bunch of Tooth's men bunched around Jack and pressed him against the rail. It looked bad... blades and knives hacking and thrusting all around. And that was when Bolton came swinging over the rail, on a grapple caught in the rigging, and dived onto the bastards from above. With his axe in his free hand, he swung down and chopped into 'em like a cleaver into meat. Laid near half of 'em low before they saw him coming.

"One man watched his chance and knifed Bolton in the back. Pa says old Bolton swung around on his heel and killed him clean, with that blade still stuck in him and blood running like water. He slipped in his own blood, and another of Toother's men came after him with Bolton's own axe, that he'd dropped.

"Pa said Bolton was on his back, but arched to keep the knife from digging in. Couldn't roll away because of the bodies on the deck. Couldn't get up...so he scooted, real fast, along the bloody planking. The axe come down, and it took off his leg in one whack. That brought Bolton up, right enough. He went sliding up against the rail and propped himself on one hip. Had his own leg in his hand, the knife still slantways in his back, and he laid into those men like a madman."

Nel gulped, his eyes wide.

Billy grinned at the effect his tale was having. "Pa says Bolton tied himself to the rail, once he got some elbow-room, and gutted anyone who got into his reach with the knife he'd pulled from his own back. When they got things sorted out, there were twenty bodies piled up around him. He near bled to death, but he's too tough to die from something like that."

"Whoo!" gasped Nel, in spite of himself, cocking his head to stare between the other boys at their teacher.

There stood Bolton on his wooden leg, his bald pate shining with exertion. He was putting one of the older boys through his paces with the saber. Holding the much younger man in check with effortless skill, the old man swung his blade tirelessly. Nel had assumed there might be a lot of exaggeration in the tale he had just heard, but now, watching the old man at his work, he wondered. Bolton might be hard-nosed old bastard. But, by golly, he was one tough Hawker.

CHAPTER SIX

Cormal hadn't planned to stay so long in Portland. Not more than a few days, at the most. Certainly, he hadn't intended to be staying a month. He'd hoped to be well away before winter came whipping down out of the northeast to freeze the ground.

That had been before he met Koola. Things had happened since then that seemed to bind his fate to that of the hairy little Macaque. Used as he was to taking things as they came, Cormal had simply let matters take their course.

The fracas at the inn had begun the real friendship. It had been a crowded night, and he and Koola had eaten their meal (generously paid for by the Macaque, who had also offered to share his one-room flat with his new human acquaintance). This inn was near his lodging, in the middle of the dock area. The two often ate and drank there.

They'd been about to drink a last mug of ale when a drunken idiot had begun pawing at Tessa, the pretty barmaid. Cormal liked the girl, and the sight had made him angry. He set his mug on the table and began to rise from his chair.

Koola caught at his sleeve. "Take care," the Macaque hissed. "See? No oth'rs do anything. You get in tr'ble!"

Cormal flushed. "You know that Tessa's no ordinary bar wench. She's caring for her ailing father and her brother. I'll not sit here and let that oaf haul her about. If the others don't care to dirty their hands with that no-good, then that's their affair. Let me go, Koola!"

He pushed back his chair and worked his way to the end of the room. Tessa was protesting quietly, struggling to free her wrist from the big paw of the drunken fisherman.

47

"Friend, I think you'd best let Tessa go, and have another drink," Cormal said quietly. "I'll buy your ale, myself. This an honest girl, no harlot."

Surprised, the big fellow loosed his grip and turned to stare at Cormal. Then, without warning, he crunched his fist into the woodsman's face. Cormal sidestepped most of the lucky blow, and said, "You're drunk. I'm sober. It wouldn't be a fair fight. Cool down, friend."

But the man had been drinking hard for a long time. Now he moved as if under water, his blow coming so slowly that Cormal had to wait for him to recover his balance before stepping forward to cuff his ears. That angered the big fellow even more. He tried to lunge at Cormal, who ducked a flailing fist and cracked the fisherman beneath the jaw with his right. The smack echoed through the inn. So did the thump as the man hit the floor and turned up his eyes, out cold.

Tessa, who had watched the fracas with a heavy crockery pitcher in hand, ready to help her defender if the need arose, went up on her toes to give Cormal a kiss. Not a sisterly kiss, either, he noted.

Then she set the tavern boys to dragging out the slumbering troublemaker. The other patrons, bravery restored, offered Cormal pats on the back, congratulations, and free ale.

Cormal found it exciting. He had never been considered a hero before, and the thing was a bit intoxicating. Koola had watched the entire affair with a calculating expression in his small bright eyes.

As they walked back to the flat, Koola asked, "You hit like that always?"

"Huh? Oh...you mean fight? That wasn't a fight, Koola. That poor fellow was drunk as a boiled owl."

"You be fighter, friend Cormal. Can see. How you hit. How you step. Is not so?"

The woodsman paused and turned to look down at Koola. "I wouldn't say that I'm a real hard-nosed fighter. I'm fairly good with my hands, you could say." He quirked an eyebrow. "Why the questions?"

"Jus' idea. Mus' think on this."

As they ambled homeward, Cormal forgot about the

48

conversation. But two days later, when they stopped at a dockside market for a dinner of honey-biscuits, the Macaque proposed his plan.

Cormal almost choked on a sticky-sweet crumb. "What are you saying? Fight someone I don't even know and have no grudge against...so you can lay *bets* on the winner? It's outrageous, Koola. Fighting's something you do when you can't help it!"

The furry head cocked to one side. The Macaque gazed up earnestly. "Is much to be made fr'm such. You good at fight. We make many arg'nts. Liv' bet'r. Have money when need."

Such a thought took his breath away. Cormal had opened his mouth to refuse, when he looked down into the beaming monkey-face and thought again. "By the hide of the Big Dog, why not? But only once, Koola. One fight. No more."

The Macaque grinned. "Good. Koola go now to fin' place. Tell people. Back soon."

As he watched the small shape scurry off toward the throng in the street, Cormal thought. One fight. A fair take of argents. No particular problem, unless Koola over matched him. As he finished his honey-cake, he mused on the quickness with which the Macaque had seized upon his fighting abilities.

In a short while, Koola was back with news. "Fight t'night. War' house on wat'rfront. Many come. You see! You ready?"

"As ready as I can be on such short notice," he grumbled. But he followed Koola down the dim street.

The place was already packed. Fishermen crowded shoulder to shoulder with traders, who in turn shoved soldiers. They filled the big space with varied stenches and curses as they jostled for a better view of the ring,

That had been marked off into a square of pallets tied together and covered with a heavy canvas tarpaulin. The moving mass cast weird shadows, as the torches in wall sconces flickered and smoked. Poor lighting, Cormal decided. But he didn't need much light. The giant in the corner of the ring could have been seen at midnight by a blind man.

His sheer bulk was overwhelming. As Cormal took his seat on a crate at one end of the mat beside Koola, he turned.

"If that monster doesn't kill me, friend Koola, remind to murder you when this massacre is over."

Koola scratched the knobby ridge above his eye. His smile didn't change. "Him big, eh Cormal? Big man. eh?"

"Big? He's a tree on feet! Look at him!"

The Macaque chittered and reached out a sinewy arm to pat Cormal's shoulder. "Big tree fall hard. He fall, too. You good fight'r."

Cormal grunted noncommittally, but Koola didn't hear him. He was busy raking in bets from all comers. The Macaque held a flat board on which he kept his tally with a sharp piece of flint. The slate filled with wagers. It suddenly occurred to Cormal to wonder how much they themselves, were wagering on this fight...but maybe it was better if he didn't know.

The giant stood and began peeling off his tunic. Cormal forgot about irrelevancies like betting. Those biceps were enough to make his skin goose-pimple.

When the bets were down, Koola skipped to the center of the ring and held up his hands for quiet. The noise died away. The little creature said, "Friends, now is fight tween Kal, free sold'r, Cormal of the woods. No rules."

He gestured. Both men came up beside him. As they came within arm's reach, Koola danced backward, leaving them face to face.

"Now, you fight;" he cried.

Cormal hadn't been accustomed to very formal fights, but this abrupt beginning made him stare at Koola in surprise. The big man's knuckles plowed into the side of his face to remind him where his attention should be. He sailed backward and landed on his rump. Shaking his head to clear away the stars dancing before his eyes, he squinted. A pair of tree-trunk legs was marching straight at him.

He's going to trample me! Cormal thought.

Kal bent from the waist. Cormal buried a fist upward in his groin. No rules? Fine!

Kal screamed and grabbed himself, giving Cormal time to regain his footing and grab the big fellow around the neck.

Locking his fingers, he drove his knee up with all his strength, hitting Kal on the forehead with a sinister thunk.

Cormal loosed his grip as the other's head snapped back. He went down, his breath harsh in his throat. Cormal dropped, knee-first, onto the exposed belly of the fallen man. He hit him solidly on the jaw. He'd show them no rules!

Kal was out of the fight for good. The crowd went wild. Those who had backed Kal were screaming about fouls. Those who had won their money were reminding them that there had been no rules, so there couldn't be any fouls. Charges of "sore loser!" were flung about, but everyone knew this had been a fight, not a social occasion. Winning had been the only goal. Cormal had reached it with utmost dispatch.

Always ready for a new sensation, Portland's waterfront took the big woodsman to its heart. Even the upper classes came, after a while, to wager on his fights in the lower town.

While Cormal wasn't quite sure how he felt about such fighting, his lazy good humor allowed Koola to continue to schedule bouts. He liked being offered drinks in the taverns. Every wench in town seemed anxious to find her way into his bed. Small boys followed him around admiringly.

He found that the tales of his wood-faring days, which he had told in taverns, his tongue lubricated by good ale, were now common knowledge among high and low. It was enough to turn the head of a much more sophisticated person than Cormal.

Each victory added to Cormal's pugilistic reputation. Strangely enough, he found no match as intimidating as the first. The troopers from the garrison seemed determined to best him, but he found them particularly easy to defeat...they were altogether too used to following rules.

That led, in time, to trouble. Cormal, surrounded by admirers after a fast and easy bout, heard a militia captain, who had lost heavily, arguing with Koola. From the man's expression, not to mention his dangerous color, Cormal thought that Koola was taking a terrific tongue-lashing. As the man lifted his hand as if to strike the Macaque, Cormal began working his way toward the pair, watching over the heads of the crowd as he went.

Luckily, several uniformed men pushed through crowd to the officer's side. As Cormal approached, he realized that the captain was one of those dangerous people who are all too used to getting their own way. Narrow eyes were filled with venom as he protested being led away. He kept glancing back at Koola and Cormal, his lips working, pulling up over his teeth and down again in a most unnerving way. He looked. Cormal thought, like a rabid dog, ready to bite anything that got into his way.

Later, at an alehouse, Cormal asked Koola about the confrontation. The Macaque shrugged. "Cap'n Slator. Bad man...could have been King in Portland. His uncle the King had no son, only daughter. Offer to make Slator heir...Slator fath'r say no. Bad man, worse King, he say. You see scar? He try to kill fath'r, when he be told. Fath'r fight, knock him into fire. Slator good man to stay 'way from." Koola drank deeply from his mug. "You see eyes?"

Cormal nodded.

"Those evil eyes. Scare Koola." The Macaque wiped the ale from his rubbery lips and said. "Not worry, friend Cormal. Drink! We make fun! You bes' fight'r in all Portland town."

And, indeed, he seemed to be. The role of celebrity was fun, too. New clothing, fine tunics and pants, with heavy leather boots, made him strut proudly. A magnificent cape made of a whole bearfox hide made him feel like a King himself. That cape proved to be valuable as a protection from the growing bitterness of the winter wind, as well as setting off his finery.

As he walked along the street one morning, Cormal noticed the iron gray of the sky. The smell of the air meant change: snow was in the air.

As he passed the outer gate of the garrison's militia compound, he paused. A dog was shrieking with pain. The guards at the gate were staring into the compound, their spears loose in their hands. Cormal stepped up to look between them. His blood chilled.

A beautiful Great Dane riding dog was staked in the center of the parade ground. It was struggling with its tethers, its powerful shoulder and haunch muscles rippling beneath its shiny yellow fur. Ropes looped about its neck were held by a pair of unhappy looking troopers. A third man wielded a whip, moving around the bound animal, beating it unmercifully. The lash laid open the glossy golden-haired hide with each stroke. The man was cursing almost as loudly as the dog was crying.

The beast's screams died to whimpers. Its eyes closed, as it tried to snap at its bonds. A snarl rose in its throat, and its hackles were up. The troopers pulled harder on the rope, half choking the animal.

One of the sentries was breathing harshly, his feelings almost out of control. The other touched him on the arm. "Don't," he said softly.

Cormal said, "Why doesn't someone stop him? What has the poor beast do to make him so angry?"

The young guard shook his head. "That's Cap'n Slator. The dog messed and he stepped into it. Nobody interferes with Slator, no matter what he does. Sometimes he puts"—the voice lowered to a bitter whisper—"one of his men out there and does the same to him. Makes sure it's someone new with no buddies and no family nearby. He does that when no other officers are on the post. Nobody can stop him...he's kin to the Queen."

Slator was still busy, the cracks of the whip echoing across the compound. Cormal could bear no more. "Kin or not, I can't stand this," he said. Before either guard could react, he was through the gate, charging across the parade ground.

Slator was so intent on his deed that he didn't hear or see the woodsman coming up behind him, hands outstretched. Those sinewy hands closed around the officer's neck. Cormal lifted him clear of the ground with a heave.

Then the officer found himself flying through the air. The ground came up and hit him, knocking a cry from his lungs. His whip was dropped in mid-flight. Cormal bent low and scooped it up. He flung it away with an exclamation of disgust.

Slator, scarlet with fury, scrambled to his feet, his fine uniform fouled with dust and dog-dung. "You...you dare to lay a hand on me?" The narrow eyes were widened with

53

rage...empty, vicious eyes. Cormal shuddered.

"Both hands, Captain. I laid both hands on you, and I'll do it again, too, if you ever lay whip to this dog again."

"You presume to tell me what I can and cannot do?" Slator's voice was shrill with incredulity. Then it dawned on him who this man was. He stepped back a pace, baring his teeth in a strange nervous way, "You! The money-fighter! The one with all the dirty tricks...who cheats honest men of their money."

Cormal frowned. "Now hold on there, you poor excuse for a toy soldier—"

"Sergeant! Arrest this man!"

Cormal realized suddenly that he was surrounded by a score of soldiers. They seemed to appear from thin air. All were armed, and many sword points were aimed at his throat before he could move. The faces above the blades were carefully impassive.

"You just wait one second," the hunter said. "I'm not in your damned army. You have no authority over me."

The men moved closer. Cormal knew that further talk was useless. He had walked into the bearfox's den this time, for certain.

"Sir!" That was a grizzled noncom with sergeant's marks on his sleeve.

"Tie him in the supply hut...in those shackles I had set into the wall. The punishment for hitting an officer is twenty-five lashes."

The sergeant looked uncomfortable. Cormal could see him controlling his impulse to tell the captain that this was a civilian...and one who hadn't exactly struck him in the first place.

"Sergeant Lanse, carry out my order at once."

"Yessir!"

"And one more thing...."

"Sir?"

"Just secure the prisoner. I'll whip him myself."

Cormal lunged past the nearest blade, punching a fast jab at its owner's face. Then he was on the next man, breaking his way through the ring of soldiers.

Nobody was going to whip him without his putting up a

battle.

But there were more soldiers closing on Cormal. He saw a sword-hilt moving at his head...and then he saw nothing.

* * * * * * *

Major Kenteen had decided, as he strode along the corridors of the Officer's Command Billets, that he much preferred his own militia fort. He and his Dogriders of First Company were not used to the stiff formality of this city post. He had been summoned to meet with General Tion. He had moved at once to comply with the orders, but he was wondering...the First had been idle for two months, since their return from the first expedition into the Canadas in almost a thousand years.

Was this a reassignment? A commendation? Or, for some obscure military reason, censure?

The general's aide met him in the hall and ushered him into his superior's office. Kenteen saluted and doffed his heavy cape.

Tion, even whiter of hair and beefier of build than when they last met, returned his salute. He waved him into a chair by the desk. "Do you know why I sent for you, Kenteen?" he asked,

"No, sir. I hope it may be a new assignment. The men hate sitting around barracks, and I don't like it much better." It was good to be able to speak frankly. Tion, unlike most high-ranking officers, expected his men to be frank with him.

The general chuckled. "But you never know if a dressing down might be in the works, either, do you?" he asked. "I know how it goes. Was in that position myself, But you rest assured, this is not a dressing-down. Your bunch did such a fine job of the Canada expedition that it won't soon be forgotten.

"Your discovery of an entire northwoods town, not to mention your trade negotiations, set the general staff on their ears. And others, too. Even higher. " The general winked.

Kenteen swallowed a lump in his throat. That meant the royal family itself had taken note of his report.

"It was a stroke of genius to bring down those people

55

from the new lands to save time with dickering. It's a tribute to you and your men that they trusted you enough to come away with you...into the blue, so to speak. That dinner we had for you wasn't just to welcome the new ambassadors. It wasn't just to announce the signing of peace and trade agreements and to announce the trade route. It was to honor you and your men. The only reason the King didn't call personal attention to you was because there are some...envious elements in the garrison, here. It might have caused more trouble than it was worth."

He looked at his desk, shifted a bit of the coarse paper made from rags and plant fiber. "Since your temporary assignment here, you've been waiting for further orders. That's just what I have for you."

Kenteen felt his chest relax.

"You can tell those Dogriders of yours to polish up their gear and get ready to head out." There was a twinkle in the general's eye. He seemed to be recalling a similar time his own career, when such news would have been more welcome.

Kenteen sat ramrod-straight in his chair. "Yes, sir! Can you tell me anything about the assignment?"

The general sat back and rubbed his chin. "I've been conferring with the rest of the general staff. We've decided that the best way to safeguard the new route into Canada is to provide secure layover points along the way. As well, we need to pacify the countryside...the few villages that exist are constantly at the mercy of bandits. We need fortified outposts along the trade route and wherever there are enough people to warrant it."

Kenteen nodded. His mind was racing ahead of the words he knew were coming.

"The King has been thinking for some time that it's time to expand our control over the wilderness to the north, the south, and the west. They believe that we should secure any parts through which travelers might need to pass regularly.

"As big as Portland has grown, the town is almost isolated by the forest all around it and the lawless element that shelters there. We're proposing that you take your men, sufficient supplies, spare mounts, along with the best guides you

56

can find, and travel a big sweep through the wilderness."

The general spread out a rough map. "Here...start off parallel to the trade route; sniff out the country. Then curve around westward and back to the south. Keep eyes and ears peeled for anybody who is making trouble or might do so later. Make contact with any groups of people you might find...hunters, trappers, small farmers. Any sized group could be useful."

The general eyed the major. "Our scouts tell us there are hundreds of tiny tribes and families and clans living there. A lot of them probably don't know they're not the only people in the world. Find them, Kenteen. Help us to pull them together. Get them to help us stamp out the villains who prey on them and will certainly play hob with anybody using the trade routes. If things work out well, some of our Portlanders may go out and settle in the newly opened land."

"Ambitious," said Kenteen.

"True. And not without its hazards, I'm afraid."

They looked eye to eye with silent understanding. Both men were aware that the outlaw groups had made that huge forest their home. It was their preserve and their hunting ground. It would not be an easy task to secure the huge expanse of woodlands.

The general spoke again. "Ever hear of a Macaque named Kray?"

Kenteen frowned. "No, sir. A Macaque?"

"Yes. A truly villainous one. Not at all like the usual sort. I was shocked when the scouts began reporting on his activities. But we have corroboration from several sources. He's smart. He's dangerous. And he has some three hundred men—an enormous force, these days—at his command. There's no way of knowing how many women and children they have back in their stronghold. Wherever that may be."

Kenteen drew a cautious breath. "Begging your pardon, but that sounds more like an army than a gang of troublemakers. The biggest single group our King can call upon is several tens less than that. Of course, if you count our entire system, we have more manpower, but it's scattered all over the map."

"It is an army...and a good one. Hit and run is his main

tactic, and that wily monkey seems to be able to vanish whenever I send out a force big enough to handle his numbers. But he's holed up in those woods. He knows them as well as I know my wife's bedroom. We're going to have to contend with him before we're through. Might as well start with him, send a message to the rest of them in the process."

"Yessir!" Kenteen felt his blood stirring from its sluggish pace of the past weeks. "We'll spy out the land, keep our ears tuned."

"Excellent. Now get over to ordnance and give them your supply list. You're to leave at sunrise tomorrow. Pick up the rest of your men at your little fort to the west, then jump off into the forest as soon as you can."

Kenteen rose and saluted. General Tion extended his hand. "Good luck, Kenteen. It's a bad time of year to send men out into the wild, but you know that. You know how to deal with it. We'll expect you back next year, by late spring or early summer. Have a good report for us!"

As he went back through the corridors, Kenteen knew from the sidewise glances he received that he must be beaming, He tried to control it, as well as his temptation to break into a trot. He had a lot to think about...and he needed expert help. Few of his men, skilled as they were, had lived in the forest or had known the sorts of people who eked out a living in the woods. He needed someone so expert that he would never have to think twice about what to do in the areas toward which First Dog was headed. There weren't many. Portlanders were city people and proud of it.

He started toward his quarters. Then, changing his mind, he went for a walk through the city. Twilight faded into darkness before he turned back toward the compound, skirting the wall that led to the royal palace, lost in his thoughts.

The compound lay beneath a full moon, which floated in orange intensity across a sky filled with high tendrils of cirrus cloud. An eerie silver light filled the parade ground. The night guards, chilled by the sudden drop in temperature after sunset, were bundled to the ears in heavy furs.

* * * * * * *

Cormal, inside the shack they guarded, was staring through one of the many crevices in the flimsy walls. He was shivering hard, partly from the cold and partly from shock. His back was raw, still bleeding from the ferocious whipping he had received at the hands of Slator.

Closing his eyes, he shuddered. The man's narrow face, with those slitted eyes filled with a light of pure pleasure, danced before his memory. The cut of the lash had been worse than the realization that here was a man who gloried in the pain of others. A nasty thought.

Warm trickles of blood were still moving down his back and sides. He jerked at the shackles again, but without hope. The post to which he was fettered was the only solid construction in the shack. Now his pain was less of a bother to him than his fury. Once he gained his freedom, that cruel-eyed monster was going to pay...and pay...and pay.

A noise...Cormal went still, hardly breathing. A scraping sounded, as if something moved against the side of the hut. A board creaked and groaned. Cormal stared into darkness, his ears trained acutely. He suddenly realized that something had appeared in the corner of the hut that hadn't been there before. A darker patch varied the quality of the blackness. Something like a small hunched figure huddled there. It moved, revealing a pale blotch that resolved itself into a pinkish face.

"Koola!" he grunted.

"Speak not loud, friend Cormal," the Macaque advised. He sidled along the wall, and from the folds of his black cloak he took a long knife. Standing on his toes, he cut through the leather thongs securing the jaws of the manacles.

"You crazy monkey! If anybody catches you here, you'll be in as much trouble as I am," Cormal whispered. Even to himself he sounded weak.

"You dumb human! Leave Koola for small-small time, what happ'n. Not blame you for get angry. But what you do, not v'ry bright. Now...you free. We go."

It took a moment to rub circulation back into his painful limbs. Then the two crept through the back of the hut where the boards were barely secured by rusted nails. The woodsman struggled through the crack into the black of the court-yard.

"We go to wall. I leave rope. We go over, dr'p into str't., then we free and cl'r," hissed the Macaque.

"You're running this show," said Cormal, and he followed silently as the Macaque flitted from shadow to shadow, making for the wall.

They had to hide several times, as guards passed on their rounds. But they reached the wall at last, and Koola scuttered up the sheer stone without exertion. Cormal waited until a rope end flipped past his face. Then, his wounds lashing him again with pain, he clambered up to the rough top and stood beside Koola.

They leaped before they heard the footsteps below. They thudded into the shape of a man, who went down beneath their combined weights.

"Damn!" choked Cormal. "Have we killed him, Koola?"

The Macaque moved. Something scratched, and a dim light shone from the Macaque's small lantern. "No. Him not dead...here. He come to!"

Cormal helped to pull the man into a sitting position. The uniform of a militia officer could be seen in the glow-worm light, and he groaned again. What now?

Shivering for lack of a shirt, he bent over the reclining officer. "Are you all right? Where do you live? We'll help you home."

"All...right," muttered the man. "Who're you?"

"Never mind that. Here, let's get you up!"

Together, Cormal and Koola helped the man to his feet and supported him as he directed them again into the compound, to his own quarters. Cormal didn't particularly enjoy going back into the den of soldiers, but he couldn't leave an injured man to his own devices.

Once inside, they saw that their victim was a major. The light from the waiting lamp revealed a spartan room, with a fire crackling in the hearth. The major sank into a worn chair beside the flames and looked at them. "I'm Major Kenteen," he croaked weakly. "What on earth happened to me?"

Koola perched on a stool and stared into the fire, leaving explanations to Cormal, who was now shaking with chill and bleeding badly. Kenteen, realizing the condition of his visi-

60

tor, rose shakily and found a blanket to put about his shoulders. "What happened to you, man?" he asked.

Briefly, Cormal told him. Kenteen listened intently, eyes darkening, contrasting with his curly shock of snow-white hair.

"Slator," he murmured, when Cormal's tale was told. "That...." he caught himself. Then he sighed and stared at Cormal. "This one is related to the royal family, so he is nothing but trouble. Rest assured that I will look into this. And that you can go in safety, from now on."

Cormal leaned back in the creaking chair. Kenteen, realizing once again that he was in pain, rose and got bandages and ointment for the lash-marks and the cuts. He bandaged Cormal tightly with strips of cloth.

When that was done, Kenteen offered him a shirt of own. "You know, I think I want to talk with you about something. I have heard the talk in town about you...you have certainly defeated enough of my troopers. They say you are familiar with the forest to the west of Portland, and even to the south. Are you?"

"Raised all over the woods," said Cormal. "I never was in a real town before until I came here. What of it?"

"I need scouts. I have been given a difficult task, and I require all the expert help I can get. Would you consider enlisting?"

Cormal folded his arms, ignoring the pain in his shoulders, "As a militiaman? No, sir, I would *not*."

Kenteen pulled at his lip. "How about joining me as a civilian scout? With good pay and a string of our best dogs as mounts? If, that is, you know the woods as well as you say."

"You sure your head is all right? We gave you a pretty good knock on it, and I think that's affecting your judgment," said Cormal.

Kenteen chuckled, then winced. "It's well enough," he said. "I have been trying to find expert woodsmen, and here you drop...onto my head, so to speak. I am soon to lead an expedition into the wilderness for the purpose of finding and noting the positions of any groups of people.

"Portland is outgrowing its boundaries. We need more

land, but we don't want to send settlers into any other group's territory. I need people who won't get lost and who can talk to those they find in language they understand. "

Cormal thought of his time in Portland. He would miss the revelry, but little else about city life. "Major, I think I'm your man. There's no woods where I'm not at home, no place I can't find, if I suspect it even exists. I can talk to anyone, either before or after beating him in a knuckle-buster. I can take you anyplace between Portland and the Canadas, over to the Yorkers, or down south as much as two months travel."

Kenteen almost clapped him on the shoulder. He re-membered Cormal's injuries and clasped his hand warmly.

Koola, meanwhile, was watching, his black eyes bright. "Hmm," he grunted. "I wond'r if Major hire more? Koola like forest. People came fr'm forest. Like to see 'gain."

Before Kenteen could reply, Cormal asked, "You really want to go? Koola, that would be great!"

The Macaque nodded. "Cap'n Slator, when he find gone, he think of Koola pretty quick. Seem smart to be where Slator not be, you think?"

The Macaque turned to look at Kenteen. "Not too good at ride dog. Major, but try to be good scout, if you say."

Kenteen recalled suddenly his conversation with Tion. Kray was a renegade Macaque, scorned by his own people. Why not set a Macaque to catch a Macaque? Fate seemed to be dealing the hands in this game.

"Done! You're hired, Scout Koola."

The Macaque danced up and down with excitement. His tail curled out from the back of his cape as he cried, "Good, eh, friend Cormal? We be scouts togeth'r!"

* * * * * * *

So when First Dog paced out of Portland, on a day of leaden skies, it was led by Major Kenteen and two strange scouts. The stragglers who had gathered to make an occasion of the departure of the troop raised a cheer for the chittering Macaque, who was trying desperately to stay in the saddle without dislocating his long, glossy tail. His companion, large and rugged, with the eyes of a sleepy panther, looked well in the homespun gray-tan of the First-Dog uniform. He was astride a spirited Great Dane and looked insufferably smug.

The gates opened and they rode out into a cold gray day. As they put the town behind them, flakes of snow began falling from the morning sky. Winter had come.

CHAPTER SEVEN

It had been a grueling year. Only Gem's hard work all her life on the farm, developing muscles and reflexes to their utmost just to survive, had allowed her to adapt to this new set of skills and disciplines.

Randor spared her nothing. Indeed, he told her frankly that he had never driven any of his male students so hard.

One day when she was soaked with sweat and beet-red with exertion, he had told her. "You haven't the weight or the reach of the men you'll meet. You have to even out the balance, you see? You have to be quicker, that's the key. Quicker to notice any flicker of the eye or twitch of a muscle that'll indicate what your opponent is about to do. Quicker to react. Quicker on your feet and with your blade. It's the one thing that can save you from even worse fates than the Hawkers managed. I'll not rest until I'm satisfied that you can hold your own with the best swordsman you'll ever meet."

To hear him talk, she would never have believed he was satisfied with anything she did. He drilled her, day after day until she could hold him at bay. He taught her everything she needed to know about archery, from curing ash for the weapon itself to fletching the arrows.

After that came long days of shooting at targets. Those were moving or resting, hidden or suddenly flashing into sight and out again. Only when she could hit them all consistently without pausing to aim did he nod and go on to work with the short stabbing knife.

Then came hand-to-hand combat. Gem was wondering if she might not die from sheer weariness before she learned all the holds, kicks, flips, and maneuvers of this most de-

64

manding of skills.

She was strong for her size and weight. She was quick, not only because of her innate ability but also because of the training in swordsmanship. Yet, if she stood toe-to-toe with her opponent, she was no match for any man larger than herself.

"So the secret, you see, is to startle him, get him off balance, befogged in his wits. Then kill him or run like mad," the old man told her. "You'll not out-power many men even of your own size. Few women's muscles can develop to that extent. Outsmart him, lass. Then outrun him. You are fast. You have fine wind. You can do both."

It was the sort of training she had prayed to find, once she had decided to go after her son. She threw herself into it with concentration. So intense was her need to do better and better that she didn't even notice the old man's increasingly satisfied look as he watched her work.

At the end of that grueling year, he said, "The time has come to try you against some'un younger and stronger in the legs than I be. We're going to the garrison. There be many a fine young cockerel there who will think you easy meat. I'll send ahead word that I've a pupil to try...they love to set themselves against those I train. It has been a long while, and they will be glad to see us."

"You believe that I'm ready?" she asked, shocked and uneasy. She wiped sweat with the back of her wrist. "I thought it would be a while yet."

"I've taught what can be done without real fighting to do. But this testing will tell me...and more to the point, it'll tell you...if you can stand up to the kind of battle you're likely to find out there in the world beyond our valley." He waved vaguely in the direction of Portland.

They went together to the garrison. Gem, dressed in her breeches and boots, looked like a boy, except for her long tail of hair. The militia officer, an old friend of Randor's named Carndel, greeted them at the gate with the measuring eye of one who bets on the racing dogs. "A likely candidate," Carndel appraised her.

Gem's stomach was aquiver with butterflies. What if she forgot something vital? What if wind or strength failed her?

Could she truly handle herself in bouts with the tough-looking youngsters she had seen in the exercise-yard?

The garrison went about its business all afternoon. Then, when the sun was just above the treetops west of the compound, the time was at hand.

Gem changed into an old tunic and breeches and a pair of boots that gripped the ground well. She retied her hair, making a club of its thickness so it couldn't hamper her motion. Then she followed Randor to the practice yard, and the first challenger.

She lulled him with parries and counterthrusts, letting him think he was controlling the pace of the bout. When he had become suitably overconfident, she made her move, sending his sword spinning away in a sun-splashed arc and nicking his shoulder.

"First blood to Gem of Dover!" shouted the sergeant.

Carndel came over to her. "Would you like to rest now?" he asked.

Gem had already shaken her head when she realized that Randor, too, was shaking his. She had come to see how she might stand up to a life-and-death battle. Such matters did not allow for time out to rest.

The second swordsman, warned by the defeat of the first, was much more cautious in his attack. They lunged and parried until both dripped with sweat and Gem's arm felt as if it might fall to the dusty ground. At last the sergeant stepped between. He knocked aside their blades.

"I call a draw. Nice work, Gem, Kandel. You're well matched. One more to go, lady. Have you the strength?"

She was gulping great drafts of air. Her legs felt like warm wax, and her chest hurt with the exertion. She nodded once again. If she could endure one more bout and come out creditably, it would prove to her that she could take chances in the wild lands with some hope of survival.

The third man was fresh. He was wily. He was skilled enough to hint that Randor might have had a hand in his teaching. He wore her down, inch by inch, though her blade wove bright patterns between them, holding him at bay. Gem's arm grew heavier by the minute. The blade itself, light though it was, seemed to weigh more heavily all the

66

time. She was almost glad to feel a tap at her arm, followed by a slow stream of blood that meant the bout could end.

"Blood!" called the sergeant. "Bout to Hanser. But very nice work, lady. Few of us would have held so long with a fresh opponent, after such demanding bouts."

Carndel's red-faced wife, who matched his own burly build, was beside her, fussing over her arm, binding it to stop the flow of blood. Over her head, Gem looked at Randor. As she caught his eye, he winked, a long slow wink and she knew she hadn't disappointed him.

The next morning's bouts were less satisfying. Close-in work with a knife that you can't use fatally is wearying and dangerous. But even those three hard-fought matches told Gem that she could have killed, if she had been in earnest, long before the end of each match.

It was in the hand-to-hand combat that she surprised herself and everyone else. Though they overtopped her by anything from four inches to a foot, the best fighters of the garrison simply could not get a hand on her. She doubled them over the toe of her boot. She slid from their grip to flip them over their own feet. She danced away from their attacks and tripped them or stunned them or elbowed them in the pits of their stomachs. The hand-to-hand combat went in her favor, though nobody was badly hurt.

Randor looked less grim than usual when she emerged from Dame Carndel's room, where she had scrubbed away her weariness with hot water and homemade soap. She smiled, and one of his grizzled eyebrows went up slightly. From Randor, that was an accolade. She felt better, bruised as she was, than she had done in a year.

As they returned homeward, Randor counted the argents he had won, wagering on her matches. He said no word of praise, but the clink of the silver was music to her ears. She began to chuckle, then to laugh heartily.

"So I have managed to pay you, after all," she gasped at last, wiping her eyes. "I should have known that an old soldier always has something up his sleeve besides his arm."

The old man frowned, but there was a spark of something like amusement in his eye. "So you did. And I'm not sorry I took you on. Few have the spunk to go out and try to right their own wrongs. Too few. I'd not turn away someone so determined, though if you'd proved to be unfit, I'd have sent you packing very soon."

She strode beside him into the clearing about his house. Without warning, the old man drew his blade and sprang at her.

A year ago, Gem would have been too stunned to react. Now her intense training took over. She leaped backward, drawing her sword at the same time to parry the vicious arc of his slashing steel. The days of combat just past seemed like the play of children...now she was dealing with a master of his art. And he was giving no leeway. This was her final test, she knew by the gleam in his eye, and she would have to beat the man who was her master.

Randor moved around the house, the hissing and clanging of their blades making the forest ring. The sun moved across the zenith and began to slide down the west. And still Gem, her legs weary and her arm made of lead, held off her formidable opponent.

At last a lucky move brought blood from Randor's shoulder.

"First blood!" she shouted, stepping back to catch her breath. Instead of pausing, as was always done, Randor lunged forward with his blade, and she managed to avoid being skewered on the point only by sheer luck. Again she was fighting for her life, and only when she found herself disarmed did Randor halt.

"Remember," he croaked, his chest heaving, "that first blood is only that...the first. The winner is the one who draws last blood!"

She knew she would never forget the lesson.

They staggered into the house, washed up, and fell into their bunks, too weary to cook or to eat. Only when the sun rose again did Gem open her eyes. The realization was waiting for her...it was time to go after Nel.

As she helped to build the breakfast fire, she said, "My son is out there, somewhere, needing me. Perhaps he is being abused. Am I ready to go?"

The grizzled brows met over the sharp eyes. "I have thought on that. If he is like his mother, I'd say he's holding his own. But it is nearly time. I don't say you're a match for any quickblade there is...that wouldn't be true. Even I never claimed to be. But you'll do. Nobody will come out of a bout with you without knowing he's been in a fight. And you know when to run—that comforts my mind. But taking off for Portland alone afoot—that troubles me. The forest is full of beasts on four legs and worse ones on two. You need a mount. You need a bit more time with in-fighting. There's a thing or two I've not called to mind, yet. But you're nearly ready."

They decided, at last, on one more hunt together. She needed bow practice, after so much concentration on other skills. Randor needed meat. They went after game, and they got more than they bargained for.

The worldwide Plague had done strange things. Animals had mutated rapidly into creatures that earlier men would not have recognized. Moose had become huge, their tempers short and furious. The bearfox had come into being, though nobody could say with certainty what combination of beasts had been their ancestors. Bulky, with a bear's fat body, they had the red coloring of foxes, with the narrow pointed faces and the quick intelligence of that breed in their alert golden eyes. But they, too, were fierce and predatory.

As the two hunters, separated by some two hundred yards, slid through the brush of the wood, they began to hear snarlings and grunts up ahead. Those grew louder as they went, though nothing was as yet in sight.

Gem whistled, and Randor replied. They drew closer together and went forward cautiously, bows ready.

Randor paused behind a thick shrub. He hissed at Gem, "Will ye look there, now?" he whispered.

It was something to see. A moose of such size that he must have been an elder of his kind was facing a bearfox almost as large as itself. The beast was at least as large as any riding dog Gem had seen. Its fangs were as long as her hand and looked as sharp as her sword. They snapped a five-pound chunk from the moose's shoulder in one quick pass as the two watched.

The moose was not idle. As the predator lunged and bit. The moose swung its heavy rack of permanent horns and laid the creature's side open to the bone. Dripping blood from its wounded ribs and its full mouth, the bearfox wheeled back to face its opponent again. Its growls and yaps were muffled by the mouthful of meat.

When the moose dropped its head to charge, the bear-fox dropped its trophy and rose on stump-like hind legs to meet the attack. That was a mistake. The moose's plate-like horny structure crunched into the bearfox's mid-section with the sound of splintering bone.

Randor's bow twanged. A shaft suddenly stood out behind the moose's left shoulder. Gem's arrow caught the wheeling beast fully in the throat. It stood for a moment, blood pouring from its wounds. Then it sank to its knees, groaning loudly.

Randor sent his next shot through an eye-socket into the brain, and the animal's head lolled forward, the remaining eye glazing with death. The bearfox, too, was dying. A strong pulse of blood from its chest told of a severed artery. Pitying the panting creature, Gem put an arrow into its heart. It, too, crumpled flat and breathed its last.

"We didn't exactly need so much meat;" grumbled Randor, slitting the moose's throat to bleed it. "Field-dressing this beast will take a day and a night. I've a mind...Gem, run to the village and tell your mother that there's plenty of good meat for the taking, if folk will trouble themselves to come after it."

Gem grinned. Randor was already cutting off his own favorite parts. There would be enough there to feed most of the families in Dover for weeks, if they dried the extra. But before she went, she bent over the bearfox. It was furred thickly for the winter. She coveted the fur. Randor, noticing her interest, grunted.

"I'll skin it out for you. It will be the very thing for sleeping on the trail. Winter's too nigh to lack warm furs for wrapping up in. Now go, younker."

She ran. When she returned in a couple of hours, most of the people of the village and surrounding farms were following her. Even important tasks could be dropped for the sake of good red meat.

Randor had by then packed his own cuts into the bearfox

hide and was ready to go. He was barely civil to the mayor when that worthy tried to thank him.

"You're doing me a favor," he said. "I'd not use so much before it spoiled, and even dried it would last me a year. Come, Gem. We'll be going."

They left along a game-trail that ran in the general direction they wanted. As soon as they could no longer hear the mutter of people about the carcasses, the old man paused and looked at Gem.

"That long-toothed beast was a sow, lass. Heavy with milk. She's got cubs near about, and not too far. A nursing bearfox will go no more than a few miles from her young. They eat more often, when they're tiny. Hers would be, I'd say from the signs, almost weaned. There'd be two, that's the size of litter they have. If we could find them, you'd have a mount when—and if—we can find the spot where she left 'em."

Gem's eyes widened. Kindly reared, any small creature could be tamed, she knew. Her mother had raised the young of every kind of beast that could be friendly companions. But bearfoxes.... "Do you want to find them now?"

"No," he said. "When they get hungry they'll begin making noise. Tomorrow we'll cast about the scene of the battle. By then the folk will be back in their own place and out of our way."

It took half the next day to locate the huge hollow log in which the sow bearfox had borne her cubs. Her tracks had meandered all over the wood as she hunted, but at last they stood at the end of the fallen tree whose roots stood higher than the houses in town. Mutters and moans of discontent could be heard in its depths.

"They're three or four arm-lengths from the big end," grunted Randor. "It's a good thing. I'd not like to have to crawl in to haul them out."

Gem found a stout length of branch. She pounded with it on the trunk. The thumping brought forth more protests from inside, but the cubs seemed to be moving. Randor nodded encouragement, and she pounded away again. Randor was waiting at the opening with stout bags.

"Enough!" he shouted at last. "Give me a hand, lass!

71

These are no kittens I'm catching."

The cubs were already the size of well-grown dogs, strong and feisty. But the light disoriented them, and they were quickly bagged.

Randor took one squirming bag, Gem the other. It was a very long walk back to the hut, and more than once they had to call a halt to subdue their wriggling burdens.

They didn't unbag the youngsters until they had eaten and rested. Then Randor untied the thong about the lip of the first sack and grasped the animal inside around the neck. Gem, ready with more thongs, whipped one about the jaws and neck as the creature's head emerged from the bag. She tied the front paws as well, then stepped back to look at their prize.

It was a handsome creature. Standing waist-high, it had the burly, sloping body of a bear, though the hind-quarters stood higher, promising a more secure seat for any would-be rider. It was covered with fox-red fur that curled tightly to make a waterproof coat, as well as a warm one. The head was longer and narrower than the bear of old had possessed. The triangular face held a very foxy expression, with sharp ears that stood upright. Only a relatively short snout marred the fox-mask. The eyes were golden-amber, and they held intelligence that might have startled anyone who knew only the prototypes of the mutated beast.

The second, smaller than its brother, was a female. They would become, at maturity, a mated pair, for that was the pattern in which the creatures had evolved.

Randor looked at them, his brow furrowed with thought. "It might be, Gem, that you could take the pair. They'll be happier so, and raising and training two would be no more trouble than one. You'd have to alternate mounts. Perhaps you might train them to hunt for you, too. That would save time, if you needed to move fast."

"I'll have to wait until they grow enough," she said. "That won't be long, and even at that, it will be so much faster when I do go—it will make up the time.... Yes, I'll do it. Mother can help, too."

"I might take up that offer of a cow," Randor said thoughtfully. "They can use the milk, and then I can give the animal back, once we're done with needing it."

Weeks passed, while Gem and her mother and the old soldier worked with the young bearfoxes. The creatures grew at an amazing rate and learned even more quickly. The sound of Matron Bere's or Gem's steps, as they brought stoneware jugs of milk, would bring the bearfoxes up, squealing in their pen. In two months they were shoulder-high to Gem. Their baby fat was turning to steely muscle. Only Matron Bere's skill at gaining the love and trust of animals kept them from turning against those who nurtured them. Gem learned a lot, in that time, about training them to her will. Soft words, gentle touches, quiet ways were required to keep from upsetting the youngsters.

"It's as well you have these beasts, if you insist on doing this mad thing," Matron Bere observed to her daughter, one day, as they stood by the pen, watching the cubs wrestle. "I will feel much better knowing you have such companions as these."

By first snow their task was done. Gem was ready and past ready. Her mounts were now as tall as they would grow, though they still would fill out with more bulk and muscle. Her weight was no burden to either of them. They had strength and stamina. She knew that the time had come to go.

Sentimental good-byes were a thing of a long ago past. Randor, at any time, had no use for them. So one morning, with snow falling in lazy flakes through the treetops, Gem packed her gear, kissed her mother, and thumped her teacher heartily on the shoulder. He turned back to his workbenches, while Matron Bere stood watching as long as her daughter could be glimpsed.

Mounted on Berry, the male bearfox, Gem rode into the forest, along the faint track leading northeastward. She did not look back, and the snow, quickening its falling, shut behind her like a white curtain.

* * * * * * *

Once the bitter gales set in from the northeast, the demanding morning swims for the boys were abandoned. From the docks Nel could see only a tumble of waves, even in the protected harbor. Out in the full swell of the ocean the small boats would have foundered. A single swimmer would have had no chance at all; he would be helpless as a chip in a mill-race.

The captains and crews sat through long days in the big hall, drinking and telling tales and coming to blows, more often than not over some minor point that one remembered as happening one way and another recalled in another.

The women were stuck in their houses, unless they braved the storm-blasts to visit neighbors. The boys worked, slowly, because of their cold-numbed hands, but incessantly. There was no thought of giving them time off for ease or pleasure.

Though the ones still young enough to go pirating scorned fishing as a stinking trade for duffers, the oldsters passed their summers in laying out long nets and gathering them in again, filling them with mingled catches for the tables of the island families. Those nets needed a lot of mending. New ones had to be made constantly, as the old ones were torn or carried away.

The boys made nets all winter, sheltered in a huge barn of a place where fires burned on the stone hearth. For all its inadequate heating and many draughts, the net-house was out of the worst of the wind and walled away from the freezing spray. As his raw hands worked with the wooden shuttle, Nel could hear chattering teeth all around him. Instead of reminding him of the cold, it made him think of those last days of scraping hulls on the beach in the full blast of the nor'-easter. By contrast, this task seemed positively luxurious.

There was a mutter of talk all day long. Repeated, tales heard from older Hawkers were combined with hair-raising stories the old grammas told with toothless relish around the hearth fires at night. But more than any others, the boys loved to tell of those things they intended to do "come spring."

Even now, Billy was talking about that very thing. "Come spring," he said in his breathless voice, "my Pa says they're going to take some of us with 'em when they sail. Trainin', Pa says. Cap'n Jack's been talkin' to all the men, and they've come around to his way of thinkin'. Whoever gets to go can stand watch and run errands and make themselves useful. We'll learn the ways of the Hawks. Pa says the ones that work best and keep their noses cleanest will be chosen to go. You better believe I intend to toe the line."

Nel's hands almost faltered in their even rhythm with the shuttle. He felt a jolt of excitement. If he could go with the ships in the spring, he might get within reach of the mainland. He didn't have to get really close...God knew, they'd taken pains enough to harden him for swimming miles and miles in rough seas.

Once he was ashore, he knew no Hawker ever born could catch him again. Kill him, maybe. But he'd not come back to Blood Island, for all One-Leg's careless good humor and Billy's friendly chatter. To be sure, he was one of One-Leg's favorites, and the pride of his regimen. Nel could outswim any of his companions in the training swims. He outran them all around the island. His nets were more firmly knotted, the work of his shuttle faster and neater, than any of his companions.

If only he could manage to be chosen...then his heart sank. That would not be easy. During the past year, Dida had taken it upon herself to keep him in constant trouble. She was bright and inventive enough to find more ways than he could ever dream of. He would return from a snatched meal, to find the net he'd spent the morning mending cut and fouled. Or she would trip him as he served in the eating hall, and he would spill some hot dish onto a hapless Hawker at a table. She seemed to be everywhere. Watch as he might, he never saw her before she struck.

One-Leg knew what was happening, but he just watched with amusement, making no move to ease the life of his charge. Nel knew he was watched more closely than any boy on the island...probably because he was the one who had tried to kill Jacker. If he were to be one of the chosen few in the spring, he would have to keep his wits. Otherwise, that scrawny girl would rob him of his chance to go.

From the corner of his eye, he saw something move quickly between two bales of cordage. Dida, he was sure. Now what could she be about? He kept one eye on his work, the other on the place where he had noticed motion. His task was not going to be easy, that was certain. But in spite of Dida and Jacker, and whoever else got in the way, he intended to be one of those on a ship that sailed from Blood Island in the spring.

CHAPTER EIGHT

Cormal fitted back into the winter-bound forest as a bearfox fits into its den. As a scout, he could range freely, as the troop circled, first approaching the Canadas, then sweeping in a curve to the west and south. He could investigate rumors or unusual tracks, omitting from his routine the rituals (witless, he thought) in which the military delighted. He was happy to get out of Portland.

Koola was, too. The atmosphere of the forest seemed to give new energy to the Macaque, as the two found tiny groups of people and marked them on their maps or followed up on rumors that had run from band to band.

They were now to the west and south of Portland, camped for the night by themselves, as they best liked to be. One night Koola took the opportunity to confide in Cormal, as they sat beside the fire. "We Macaque useful to humans. They need us warn of Hawk'rs. We like city, too—food, drink, arg'nts. But we feel strange, too. Man smile and still hate us...we diff'rent. We not men. Some men catch Macaque in secret, do terrible things. Most not. But some think we beasts."

The Macaque paused, then, "Make life exciting, sometime. Forest is good, though. Any bearfox eat you, if get chance. Not so with men. Some good, make friend. Some not good. Kill you quick. Is less confusing in woods—more peaceful."

Cormal gave a grunt of laughter. While his problems were not those of the Macaque, he recognized the pattern. In a place where everything was dangerous, you were never fooled. You knew enough to keep your eyes open all the time and to cover your back. In cities you often forgot those vital matters. Cormal had not forgotten his ordeal at Slator's hands.

"We make a team, sure enough," he said. He pushed a glowing branch back into the small campfire between them. "Neither of us belongs between walls, Koola. That's a fact. I was getting fat and lazy, even with all that fighting. I like this fine, though we haven't made as much headway as we should have done. Not a soul in that last village that had been attacked would admit having seen Kray or his bunch, and it's nearly a year since we started on his trail."

He scratched his chin, as if reminded of their long fruitless trek through the north woods during the last months. His curly, panther-hued beard had grown ragged and wild. "Seems like we're chasing a ghost."

Koola chuckled. "You talk to wrong people. You an' Kenteen talk to head-man, to heal'r-woman. You ask them, they shake heads, no, no, see no ren'gade Macaque. No troublemak'r. Houses burnt, people wounded, but no trouble. Never admit. Like yest'rday."

He curled his long, glossy tail around a knob of the boulder and shook his head. "Yest'rday I go to childr'n there. Macaque small, like child. Little ones talk, talk, talk to me. That village back there...they see too much ren'gade. Band raid 'em four days ago. Take off old head-man. Many oth'r... young women to sell or trade, children to train to be more ren'gade. "Band went northwest. Boy in village tell me he followed for long way...his mama carried off with 'em."

Cormal tensed with excitement. He kept forgetting how shrewd Koola could be. He and Kenteen had never thought to talk with the children. "But why didn't they tell us? We could go after them and get back those taken away!"

Koola looked up, his eyes sparkling in the firelight. "We soon gone. Ren'gade always here. Maybe we catch, maybe not. If we not catch, they know somebody tattle...they go back to village and punish. Make no diff'rence if it right village; punish all. Carry off many, kill more. You want to bet odds?"

Cormal stared into the fire. "I see. But Kray is always one step ahead of us. What can we do but pick up his tracks?"

78

The Macaque nodded. "Must get away from village. Come from diff'rent direction. Head south, circle around their main camp, eh? Tell Kenteen. Plan big strike. Those ones, they must be stopped here. Or one day, come right into streets of Portland, then what?"

Cormal met Koola's gaze. "We'll make tracks for Kenteen at moonrise. They have a long start. Lucky it hasn't snowed heavily yet." He rolled up his blanket, while Koola buried the fire beneath a pile of snow.

The snow had grown deep in the past weeks, but they made good time. Their dogs had thick coats of fur to keep them warm, with clawed pads which gave them a fine grip on ice or snow. Nor did their mounts go hungry, for they could hunt down their own food. No one had to waste packroom for grain or fodder for them. They were far more mobile in winter forays than the cavalry mounted on horses in the old days.

The next afternoon Cormal and Koola found Kenteen. He had completed a quadrant of the search pattern and was turning at an angle to tackle another area. He halted his small troop at Cormal's whistle.

The word of Kray's village raid was the first reliable break in the wall of silence that had impeded their search. Kenteen sent out riders along the other quadrants to bring in the rest of his troops. By nightfall all were gathered, and Kenteen agreed with the Macaque's plan.

They rested most of the night. Then they ate a cold breakfast and rode out into the deep snow as dawn was breaking. At last Kray was within range. They hoped.

Making a wide arc, they circled the small village from which the captives had been taken. They examined the terrain closely as they swung south before heading again to the north. Even after such a long while there might be some trace of the passing of a large group.

This was where Koola came into his own. Cormal had discovered that the Macaque could spot a displaced twig, a slight scrape against the bark of a tree, any slight deviation from the normal. His eyes were sharp, and, most amazingly, he could detect the odor of dog droppings that were as much as two weeks old...even beneath deep snow. In half a day, he found the direction the raiders had taken.

Kenteen was impressed, Cormal could tell. "You two cast ahead of us. Check out the country for any sign of the captives. One of them might have had the sense to leave some sort of clue for rescuers to follow. Mark any deviations of the trail so we can follow fast without tracking. And good luck!"

Cormal had been chafing at the slow pace of the main detachment. This new assignment was to his liking. He and Koola urged their dogs through the snow-laden forest at a good clip. Once they had taken up the trail, he found that he, too, could spot tiny signs of their passing. They made excellent time, and sundown found them far ahead of the troop.

"There are some farming settlements up this way," Cormal told Koola on the second day out. "There is a little place called Dover, and other villages along the river. Maybe Kray is scouting another raid. If we don't catch up with them first."

The two pushed their mounts to cut down the lead of the raiders, but a half-day's journey on they discovered strange traces in the forest that made them halt. Before them was a clearing where the snow was stirred and scuffled. Blood stained patches of it, as well as the bark of several trees.

Casting about, Koola found other signs. "See...some one in tree...here...shoot into raid'rs as they come. Got some, too. Good shot with bow. Raid'rs send out bunch to spy who attack 'em. Find track where ambush'r leave tree." He pointed. "There! Good track, v'ry small boot. Big boots overlay it. Come!"

They hurried along the markings that only the Macaque could have unraveled from the old tracks in the hardened snow. Suddenly the Macaque paused and bent to sniff a tree-trunk. He sniffed a tuft of winter-dried grass thrusting above the drifts. "Bearfox here. Two bearfox...one male, other female. Wait here long. Not norm'l for bearfox to stay in one place. Hmmm."

He scurried in a circle, reading the signs with eyes and nose. "One who runs come straight here. Bearfox go. Now no trace of runn'r. Only big boots go tramp, tramp around, look for one they hunt."

He looked up at Cormal, his monkeyish eyes bright. "You ev'r hear of someone ride bearfox?"

Cormal grunted and hunkered down beside a small pile of droppings. "No doubt of it. A mated pair, I'd think, but very young. See...the size of the droppings isn't nearly as big as mature beasts would leave. Small-boots comes directly here. Then no more small-boots at all. You're right, Koola. Someone has tamed a pair of the beasts for riding. Nice trick. But tough!"

Koola stood. "Go back...see where raid'rs go from here," suggested the Macaque. They turned back toward the main trail.

At the point where the attack on the raiders had started, they had abruptly changed their path. This suggested that some had been wounded and that the main force was heading back to shelter. The trail moved westward, away from the route toward the settlements along the river. It wasn't long before Koola could tell that the bearfox rider had also altered course and was following the raiders.

"We couple days behind, now. Captives slow 'em down lot. Then Small-boots give 'em trouble, too. Troop come fast, we might take 'em soon after they get to main *camp*," Koola suggested.

Cormal agreed. He attached a note to his daily mark, left for Kenteen's other scouts. Then he urged his dog after Koola's. The tireless dogs forged their way through the snow almost playfully. When loosed to hunt, they frisked away, sometimes having a fight in the snow on their way into the forest. Soon Cormal would hear their deep voices belling after their prey. When those were silenced, he knew some luckless ermine or hare had come to a sudden end.

While the dogs rested, Cormal and Koola also dozed, though they had eaten their own ration of dried meat as they rode. Before moonrise they were moving again.

When dawn turned the east to pewter, Koola whispered, "Something ahead. Close. I go see...."—and he was gone, climbing into the branches above him.

Cormal dismounted and tethered the dogs to a bush. Then he eased himself forward through the tenuous light. Only a faint crickling sound among the high branches told

81

him that Koola was overhead. Then there came a crash, gasped curses, and a thump. Something hit the snow off to the right. Cormal gripped his sword-hilt and moved forward cautiously.

"Come help, Cormal!" Koola's voice whined. "Got more than can handle!"

Now Cormal could see a wriggling heap in the snow. He pounced atop it and caught a handful of leather. Another handful of fur. A wristful of teeth. The creature in his grasp exploded into action, and he found himself fighting someone too slippery to hold and too fierce to let go.

Then Koola, now relieved, brought the battle to an end with a well-applied tap from the haft of his short-sword.

The attacker slumped, unconscious. "Small-boots," Koola guessed aloud. "Think we raid'rs." He turned the fur-clad shape over in the snow.

"A woman!" exclaimed Cormal. They stared down, astonished. "I've heard of a very few who could fight like that, but I never met one before now. That's not the sort of wrestling I prefer doing with a female!"

The woman stirred. Then she grunted and sat up. She massaged the back of her head as she stared up at the pair. Her eyes narrowed as she surveyed the Macaque. "What in creation are *you*?"

Koola was amused by her surprise. He widened his already generous mouth in a toothy grin. He stepped back to bow, his tail whipping straight behind him, holding his black cloak in a rooster-tail. "Frontier scout Koola, at your s'rvice."

Cormal laughed at her expression. "He's a Macaque. One of the monkey-people. He had the same effect on me, the first time I saw him."

She shook her head slowly, still affected by the blow. "Well, you're definitely not with *them*." She cocked her head toward the raiders' course. "That's militia gear you're wearing."

He nodded. "We're scouts for First Dog Company, out of Portland town. The question is: who are you? Why are you stalking a swarm of the toughest bandits in the woods?"

She stretched her legs, shook snow from inside her calf-high boots, and stood, pulling her cloak around her. "I'm Gem, from the village of Dover. Student of Randor. Why I hunt outlaws is my own business."

The note of warning in her voice was clear. Cormal didn't pursue the question. "It's just that we are out here doing a nasty and dangerous job. Can't have folks getting in our way."

"I don't get in anyone's way. I can handle myself in any situation."

Cormal nodded agreement. "You certainly have demonstrated that." He stared at the scuffled snow where she had battled Koola. She grinned, and he discovered that she was much younger than he had thought. And prettier. He pitied anyone making the mistake of thinking her fair game.

"I'm sorry if I hurt you," she said to Koola. "I thought you were raiders, doubling back on the trail. I've been following this bunch for days."

"We see. Drew blood, eh?"

"I put arrows through a couple of the bastards from the trees, before they knew what hit them. They've taken captives...some women and several small children."

Cormal nodded again. It bore out their interpretation of the signs in the snow. As he listened to the woman, he found himself liking her. A lone female who would chase a band of cutthroats wasn't something you encountered every day.

She interrupted his thoughts with. "All right. I've told you who I am. Now who are you?"

"Cormal," he said. "From the forest to the west. Beyond the mountains."

Koola laid a hard hand on his arm and squeezed. "Quiet! Listen!"

Cormal and Gem stared at the Macaque, as he set a long finger across his lips. His head turned slowly, as he surveyed the surrounding trees. Cormal's dog sniffed the air and growled, baring his fangs. Gem's hand moved to her sword-hilt. They all heard a rustle in the snow-thick bushes. There came a familiar twang.

"Down!" Gem cried. She tackled Cormal and flung him, head-first, into the snow.

Loud slaps sounded above their heads. When Cormal

turned his head, he saw Koola pointing to the spot where the man's head had been a heartbeat before. Two arrows vibrated in the oak tree, their feathers still moving.

Raiders boiled out of the woods. They were mounted, swords in hand, and screaming war-cries as they came.

The three had been caught in a well-executed ambush. They all realized immediately that their chance of survival depended upon instant action. Cormal rolled one way, Gem rolled another. Both came up with blades drawn to meet oncoming attackers.

Gem ducked a blade that whistled over her head. Jerking her weapon upward, she drove her point beneath a raised arm, into exposed ribs. The thrust penetrated the thick fur clothing the outlaw wore. He spasmed in agony as she pulled her weapon free. His dog ran from beneath him as he toppled, dead before he hit the snow.

Koola dodged a charging dog, skittered under the legs of another, while fending off blows that seemed to be falling like rain. He needed space! He drew his hunting knife and leaped onto the back of a passing raider. The startled outlaw tried to reach the strange, vicious thing on his back, but Koola clung like a burr. He cut the man's throat with a single stroke. Hastily pushing the corpse aside, he reached for the loose reins and guided the yapping mount beneath a tree. He reached up to grasp a branch, and within an eye-blink he had disappeared into the needled treetop.

Cormal found himself between two dog-riders, working in tandem. They had evidently fought together regularly and knew exactly how to keep him penned. No matter how he maneuvered, his back was to one of them. They were grinning as they prepared to finish him off.

The scout's lips drew back from his teeth. He scooped his own knife from a leg-strap and flipped it to rest the tip between the fingers of his left hand. With his right he maintained a wall of steel blade between himself and his attackers.

The first rider struck downward. Cormal caught the blade on his own with a zing of steel. Kicking upward with his right leg, he caught the dog beneath the flank, sending it leaping with pain.

With his primary foe busy trying to manage his dog. Cormal twisted just in time to avoid a thrust from number two. His head whipped back, but he felt the kiss of steel on his cheek. Too close by far! He threw his knife with a flick of the wrist. The blade spun between him and his enemy. The raider watched in horror, his eyes wide as targets. The knife quenched its glitter in one of them.

Cormal didn't stand still to admire his work. The moment the knife left his hand, he sprang toward Gold, his Great Dane. The beast had waited with iron discipline for a clear order from its master. He reached his mount as the first of his attackers regained control and came after him. Without slowing, Cormal leaped to hook a leg over Gold's back. Even as he gained the saddle, the dog moved to avoid the charge.

"Get 'em, Gold!" Cormal shouted.

Gold bared his teeth and went for the other dog's throat. The beast twisted to avoid the fangs, its ears laid back, ruff raised at the back of the neck. Cormal, who had witnessed many dogfights, had never before been a part of one. As the beasts lunged and snapped, he and the outlaw had all they could do to stay mounted. Mini-cyclones of teeth and fur, the two twisted round and round in the snow, trying for a death-grip.

Meanwhile, Gem pirouetted to avoid a lance, feeling the shaft brush her cloak as she turned. It missed by an inch. She lashed out at an approaching dog, slashing its hind quarters. The animal yelped and leaped, sending its master sprawling onto his back. Before he could get back on to his feet, Gem aimed a thrust at his face. The blade tracked across the pale features and found the throat. The man gurgled and fell back. She whirled to meet the sounds of another attacker.

She was too late. A dog hit her full on, sending her reeling. "Too many!" she said as she fell. She rolled onto her elbows and stared up into a snarling muzzle right over her. She had no time for any move at all.

"Eeeeeyah!" A ball of dark fur and fluttering brown cape dropped from the tree, blocking the charge of the big Boxer dog. At the unexpected motion, the animal veered, while the outlaw riding him fought to bring him back toward his prey.

Gem, on her knees in the snow, grunted. "Thanks!" she yelled.

"Okay, Small-boots. But h'ry. Don't want die on back, eh?"

She put two fingers to her lips and whistled shrilly. Koola cupped his empty hand over his left ear. "You make me deaf besides dead?" he asked.

Before she could reply, they were knee-deep in more outlaws. Koola fell back against the tree and tried to assess their opposition. They'd killed six or seven. Still there were raiders everyplace he looked. The only advantage he and Gem had was the smallness of the clearing, which limited the number of mounted attackers able to approach at any one time. He knew it would be only a short while, though, before they were all cut down.

As the monkey-man thrust and parried, he felt Gem at his back, holding her own attackers at bay. Then there came through the din of yelping and clashing steel yet another sound. He had heard it only a few times in his life. A growling roar shook the trees...an angry roar exploding from the forest on two sides of the clearing. Two huge bearfoxes, their coats glowing redly against the snow, came trampling from the trees.

One crashed headlong into two dogs, bowling both over and spilling their riders into the drifts. Before the two riders could rise, vicious claws slashed left and right. Steely fangs buried themselves in their flesh. While the teeth of the bear-foxes were dismembering the men, their rear paws were slashing the two attacking dogs to ribbons. Then the beasts lumbered on, seeking vengeance on those who wanted to harm their master.

Koola found that his adversaries were so shaken and dis-tracted by the fates of their fellows that he could make quick work of them. Then he leaped forward to stab another rider, pulling him down from his dog.

Merry, the bitch bearfox, went up on her hind legs and swiped the head from a running dog. Its rider registered shock...in the instant before he, too, was lifted into the air and sent flying by a second swipe. His mangled body hit a stout pine tree and slid bonelessly to the ground.

Delivering a final blow to a Dalmatian, Gem looked about. Her pets might well kill her new acquaintances before they learned that these were not the enemy. She pulled the Macaque behind her, and shielded him, just as he stepped from behind a wounded dog that had fallen her feet.

"Small-boots, you call for those?" he asked, pointing with his bloody knife toward the raging bearfoxes.

"Yes, they're mine—or I'm theirs."

"Good. Koola think he maybe be dessert. After they eat up all raiders. Much scary, you think?"

She dodged a fleeing raider and laughed. "We'd better find Cormal! Merry and Berry don't know he's not the enemy."

She looked about and spotted a swirl of battle that marked Cormal's position. "Friend!" she shouted, as Berry obediently wheeled in that direction.

Dogs and men were now scattering desperately into the forest. They were trying their best to flee the bearfox, and the confusion had become pandemonium. Adding to the nightmarish quality of the scene, chunks of men and dogs were being flung into the air as the bearfoxes forged their way through the press.

Gem and Koola found Cormal caught in a squeeze between a German Shepherd and his own Great Dane. The two dogs dribbled blood from their jaws. Their hackles were up, their ears laid back, blood-lust in their eyes.

Even as Gem came on the scene, Gold lunged and caught the shepherd by the throat. Twisting his head, he tore open the neck and pulled. The shepherd staggered, tried to lift its head, and collapsed at Gold's feet. The rider of the vanquished dog scrambled to his feet and ran through the blood-spattered snow. In his panic, he ran directly into one of the bearfoxes. Too late, he realized that doom awaited him, paws outstretched. The man screamed. Then the powerful beast folded him to his bosom. The man's blade scratched a bright track across Berry's belly. Enraged, the bearfox crunched his head between powerful jaws.

The three watchers just looked away. Even a hardened warrior didn't relish such a gruesome sight.

Koola and Gem picked their way across the fouled snow to Cormal's side. "Cormal! You okay? We fine. Bearfoxes friends to Small-boots. Just in time, they come. We okay now. We win. For now."

That seemed an understatement to Cormal. The pair of beasts had, in a few raging moments, torn the enemy ranks apart. Only three had escaped and were racing through the woods, but Cormal was annoyed that any had gone free.

"Koola, get your mount. We've got to catch them!"

Gem watched him as he checked Gold's wounds. When he found none deep enough to cause immediate concern, he turned to answer her unspoken question.

"We have to stop 'em before they warn Kray. He's their leader, and he's hidden out in the mountains. If anyone gets through to warn him that troops are searching, we'll lose any chance at surprise."

She wiped her blade clean in the snow. "You're right. There are still captives, too, don't forget that. Who knows what will happen to them now?"

Cormal frowned. Those fleeing men might be capable of any atrocity. The girl interrupted his thoughts when she moved between the bearfoxes, still savaging the remains of their victims. She spoke in soothing tones as she examined Berry's cut. She drew a packet from the saddle on the smaller animal and anointed the wound.

"It's not so bad, Berry. I'll fix it up well, as soon as I can. Now we have to ride with these new friends." She reached to pat the bearfox between the ears. As she did so, she motioned for Cormal and Koola to come closer.

"These are friends, my dears. My friends and yours. Don't hurt them or their dogs. All right?" She took Cormal's hand, which he offered rather less than enthusiastically, and held it near the beasts' noses.

The furry masks showed no expression, yet the eyes were alert. Merry seemed to growl at Cormal's bearfox fur jacket, and when Gem set Koola's hand at his nose, Berry gave a muttering grumble that sounded much like a question.

She laughed. "Yes, this one is strange. Not like me or Cormal. He's a friend, just the same."

The bearfoxes stood quietly as Gem led the scouts and

the dogs around them, letting them get their look and their smell fully into their senses. When she was done, she caught her saddle-loop and sprang into place on Merry's back. The dog mounts continued to shift and growl uneasily.

"I think our dogs will take a while to adjust to your... pets," Cormal commented, as she pulled up alongside them.

"Maybe if I ride ahead they won't be so nervous," she suggested. "Besides, Berry and Merry can move more easily through the mud and slush and snow."

Cormal nodded. "Ready, Koola? We'd better get on our way. They've got a good start, already."

Gem nudged Merry and gave her her head. The bearfox took off at a ground-eating gallop through the trees, leaving Gem to fend for herself when it came to overhanging boughs. Cormal and Koola came behind, pushing their dogs to full speed as the big beasts ahead located a recently trodden game trail.

Cormal noted the track with interest. He was certain marauders knew hundreds of similar routes through the forest, routes nobody else would know. He made frantic mental notes of landmarks and changes of direction. When he returned, First Dog would learn from his memory.

Koola bumped and bounced. Riding dogback was still agony to his tail, as well as his kidneys, despite all the months of jouncing in the saddle. Macaques were not built for sitting on dogs, but he gritted his teeth and hung on. He was determined to last, whatever his own discomfort. Nevertheless, he was praying to his ancient and nonhuman gods for some respite.

As luck would have it, his prayers were answered. In less than an hour, the pursuers came upon a small frozen pond. It had been the scene of yet another desperate conflict.

Tearing through the fringe of forest around the clearing at the pond, the three panicked a group of haggard survivors. These were not raiders...they seemed to be remnants of the captives that were being herded back to Kray's headquarters.

Gem dismounted and sent her bearfoxes back into the woods. Then she extended her hands, palms up, toward the weary crew and edged forward.

The captives were in the last stages of freeing themselves from their ropes and chains. Two of the raiders lay on the ice. Their exhausted dogs were crouched on the snowy bank, whining over their lifeless masters. There was no sign of the third man who had escaped the ambush on the scouts.

A scrawny woman came forward, holding a sword ready in her hands. She studied Gem closely before making up her mind not to raise it. "Will you help, lady?"

"Of course," Gem said. "We came for that, as well as to hunt the outlaws."

Cormal and Koola were busy cutting away ropes from the ones still bound. The adults had been bound cruelly tightly, and even the children had lost circulation in wrists and hands. As he helped to massage the blood back into numbed limbs, Cormal found himself wondering how the five women and eight children, bound as they had been, had managed to attack the two armed men successfully. The thin woman, whose name was Jace, was anxious to tell their story. As they kindled fires and set dried meat to simmering for the tired and hungry group, she began the tale.

"We're a trade family. Though we're not all related, of course. Traveling traders do a lot of intermarrying and changing around as we meet on the trails or visit villages. The outlaws raided our camp a while back—I've lost count of the days—and took a good twenty of us.

"In a while, they brought in some more from another village. There are fewer of us now because they killed the youngest children and knocked the injured women in the head when they couldn't keep up," She closed her eyes and caught her breath. Her bloodless face turned paler.

"The ones you see here came through that forced march through the woods. They gave us just enough food to keep us alive. To be honest, they weren't doing any hunting for themselves, either. They seemed in a rush to get where they were going—someplace up in those mountains." She pointed toward the peaks Cormal knew were ahead, though at the moment, they were hidden behind the encircling trees.

"Our kind has traveled these woods and the edges of the high country for generations. There are caves in those heights that could hold an army."

Cormal said thoughtfully, "So it's likely that Kray has

90

made his command quarters up there. And that whatever cave he has chosen is one that can be easily defended. He's no fool, whatever else he may be. Do you have any idea how far it is to the mountains?"

Jace considered carefully. "Three days, going full out. Five if you spare your beasts." She stirred the potful of simmering meat. "Anyway, a couple of days ago we were struggling along when arrows came out of the trees and killed a couple of the raiders. They scared the rest, too. They began to run us even harder. They decided, finally, to tie us up here and go on the back trail to set up an ambush."

She laughed. "They didn't leave any guards with us. They don't think much of women and children. They had warned us that if we moved a peg they'd hunt us down and kill us all. Slowly. There wasn't much we could do, tied as we were. They rode out. After a while three of 'em came galloping back as fast as their beasts could move. They were scared green, I tell you." She tasted the broth and stirred the pot faster.

"They goosed us to our feet, trying to get us to run ahead of 'em, but you could tell they weren't paying close attention to what they were doing. They kept looking back." She held her hands over the crackling fire and rubbed them together gratefully. "They tied the women together, three in one file, two in another. All the children were strung together like perch on a line. Anyway, Grace and I were on the double coffle. We looked at each other, knew what was in our minds without saying a word, and turned on the raider who was herding us along. We took him off his mount with the slack of the rope and killed him with our hands." She laughed shortly.

"The others saw what we'd done and served the other the same way. The third got his dog moving just in time to get away from us. Last we saw, he was riding north as if all the fiends were behind him."

Cormal patted her thin shoulder. "You have a right to feel proud. Not many would have thought so fast or acted so promptly. Your clan will be glad to get you back." He turned to speak to Gem, but she was gone.

She was kneeling among the huddle of children, examining them with care, looking into faces, tousling hair. Koola stood near, watching her with a puzzled expression.

Cormal went to stand beside the Macaque. "Something wrong?" he asked.

"Something about Small-boots. Nag at shadow-place in head. Something remind me...no. Cannot recall right now. You want something?"

Cormal nodded. "You ride back to intercept the major. "Tell him what has happened. We'll make camp here and wait for you to bring him back with the troop. And hurry, my friend."

The Macaque bobbed his furry head, rubbing his back-side with one hand. "Koola go fast. Back soon. More dog-ride...oh, my!"

He turned to skitter across the ice. Halfway across, he purposely slipped, skidding the rest of the way on his back, his funny boots waving in the air. The children, already intrigued by the Macaque, giggled. Koola grinned foolishly, regained his feet, and sprang onto his waiting dog. He rode away with a flourish of his cape.

Gem now returned to Cormal's side. "We need meat," she said. "Not only for these people, but also for the troop when it gets here. I'll keep the fires going and make a good bed of coals if you'd like to hunt for something big and juicy."

"Good idea." He turned to the waiting Gold, who was scratching at a flea behind his ear.

"Don't get lost!" Gem called teasingly.

"Hah! The day Cormal gets lost is the day you'll wear a dress and faint at the sight of blood."

She reached for a handful of snow to throw, but he was on his way, laughing.

* * * * * * *

A watcher, high on the cliff above the entrance to the cavern housing Kray's renegades, shouted to warn of an approaching rider. Nadar, second in command to the marauding Macaque, hurried out onto the apron of stone before the arched entryway. He glanced back nervously, hoping that his chief was still busy in the depths of the complex of caverns. Kray had been angry that morning. When he was angry, any problem at all made him worse.

A rider was now visible, crossing the stream that edged the flat area before the cave. He looked terrible—blood had dried on his filthy clothing. His dog was wounded, too, and it limped as it walked.

Nadar gestured to two men, who went forward and dragged the dirty, half-starved man from his dog. The animal, relieved of its burden, gave a short gasping howl and fell dead. Nadar looked down. "Get rid of that carrion!" he ordered.

He had two of the slaves haul the messenger, a man named Lan, into his own quarters, hoping that the disturbance would not bring Kray to investigate. A captive woman came with water, which she dribbled into the slack mouth of the injured man.

When his eyes opened, Nadar stared into them and said, "Tell me!"

The man's eyes rolled wildly in his grimy face. Terror was there, along with his pain. He had begun his stint with the renegades as a captive hunter. He had joined the band voluntarily, hoping to escape the dreary life of drudgery that was the fate of those the renegades brought back from their raids. But he knew too well the penalty for failure among those he had followed.

"All gone. All the raiding party," He gasped and gripped his side. "We had captives...going along good. A bowman stalked us...shot two. Followed...." His voice trailed off, and Nadar gestured for the woman to bring wine.

"He followed us," Lan said, his lips red with the wine. "We sent back a group to ambush him, leaving women and children. We got...slaughtered...Bearfoxes came....

"Only three lived, then. And after, only one...was left to come with the word." He rolled onto his side, groaning with pain.

Nadar looked down contemptuously. He motioned to the armed renegade at the door. A thrust ended the wounded messenger, and the woman tugged the corpse out of the rock-hewn chamber, leaving a trail of blood.

It was bad news. Kray did not accept such gladly. Nadar always had the uneasy feeling that he might be served as he had served Lan, just now, when he took such news to his master. He made his way through the immense caverns, passing clusters of his henchmen, lines of captives who were carrying in water from the stream or bent beneath the big buckets of garbage that had to be removed from the caverns every day. Some still had the strength and the nerve to shrink from him, which was gratifying, but most were too beaten down even to notice as he stalked past them.

Yet the sight of so many who were subject to the will of Kray cheered Nadar. There were hundreds of people in the caverns, and at least half were outlaws of his own kind. The rest were nothing, farmers or small hunters, frightened out of their wits. He smiled as he hurried down the stony corridor. No small setback could possibly bring down the empire that Kray was building here in the edges of the mountains.

Kray was, as he had known he would be, angry...too angry to speak, his charged silence making his lieutenant more uneasy than verbal abuse might have done. It was like waiting for a storm to strike...threatening clouds in the distance, flashes of lightning, all far away. You knew that it would lash you, eventually.

He followed as the Macaque paced the caverns. Men cowered in their billets, dreading his rage. Slaves, captured over the years, slunk silently away from his path, fearful for their lives. Nadar knew that nothing but wits and strategic talents kept Kray at the top of this heap of cutthroats. Until the Macaque had come, they had been disorganized rabble, tiny bands that hit and ran, hiding in the forest. No leader had possessed the ability to weld them together and to rule them.

Kray had welded them into a cohesive unit. He taught them the strength of numbers and the usefulness of discipline and daring. Now they had loot and slaves beyond any dream they had ever entertained. Not one of his henchmen ever considered trying to take his place. His leadership was a necessity.

For years the outlaws had lived a trouble-free existence in what they had come to regard as their unchallenged domain. The intelligence network Kray had woven through the woods and mountains assured that nothing moved without being reported by his scouts.

Kray had been informed long before that a dog-riding force had entered his territory. They came from the northeast, he assumed from Portland. He was miffed that such a distant town would take it upon itself to meddle in his empire. The effrontery irritated him, but not sorely. What could they possibly accomplish?

Others had come before. The size of this force would be hindered by the thick pine forests, he knew from earlier feeble attempts by local militias. This would be no different. After a winter in the wild, the Portland riders would scatter home, beaten and weary from chasing ghosts. Still, Kray had made it a point to keep the troops under scrutiny.

Now the unbelievable had happened. The dog troop had disappeared from the renegades' observation. No scout, no spy could find them. Somehow, the commander was using his mobility as it should be used, as a tactic to befuddle his enemy.

Now, instead of an intelligible report, the Macaque had received a garbled account from a lone survivor. One of his most skilled parties of raiders had been destroyed completely. Never before had his forces met such defeat, and the event left Kray's mouth tasting sour and foul. It was a threat to their power, unlike any before now.

Kray was thinking feverishly, trying to decide on a way to counter the dog riders. They held a numerical advantage, Kray knew from early reports. The raiders, however, were not trained militia. They lacked the drills, the in-depth training in fighting techniques that the troopers had. In an all-out encounter, Kray feared the difference might spell defeat.

"We cannot go head-to-head with dogboys," said Kray finally to Nadar. "Small, quick strikes leave 'em confused. It's the way. Hit and run, hit and run, until they're scared and scatt'red. Hide in woods, wait for chance, then strike. If not... too bad f'r us!" He stared meaningfully into Nadar's eyes.

Their base was well hidden. The soldiers in the forest were simply a nuisance, to be dealt with as usual. Kray would not consider anything else. Kray cracked his hands together. "Find off'cers!" he snapped.

Nadar relaxed. Kray was still angry, but now he was in control again. A plan was forming in his monkeyish head. Kray's men were masters of hit and run. It was the natural tactic of murderers and thieves. Soon their foes would regret trespassing on their turf.

CHAPTER NINE

When Koola rode in with his report, Major Kenteen's eyes lit with purpose. In minutes, he had First Dog mounted and on the move. Koola rode beside the major, filling in the details of the skirmish and the rescue of the captives. By dark, the troop had come to the camp at the pond. Kenteen looked about in the twilight, his gaze searching out defensible positions.

"Not a good site, from a strategic standpoint," he said. Then he looked again at the bedraggled captives and sighed. "But it will have to do. These people can't go any farther. It'd be cruel to try to make them."

As the men made camp, he moved among the former captives, learning names, ages, everything he could about each one. Then he put them in the charge of Sergeant Lanse. "See to them, Lanse. Food, any clothing we can scrape up from the gear. Be sure they're kept warm and in the center of the camp, where they'll be safe from anyone sniping from outside the ring."

Jace, who stood nearby, took his hand, stood on her toes and kissed him. It embarrassed the major considerably. But she had turned to follow the Sergeant and didn't see the blush showing through Kenteen's tan. Gem, however, saw, and she hid her smile.

She had immediately liked the officer and understood why Cormal and Koola held him in such respect. She had paid close attention to him at their first meeting, when he questioned the three about the ambush in the forest. She knew that he had doubted some of Koola's report, until he had seen Berry and Merry with his own eyes. Even now he was watching them wrestling on the opposite bank of the creek that fed the pond. She went to stand beside the officer.

"They won't attack unless I order them to," she reassured him. "I raised them from babies. I'm their mother, they think. They still aren't full grown, and it may be that as they mature there will be a problem, but that's a long way off. And it may never happen."

Kenteen smiled. "This is not what I'd call a normal campaign." He signaled to Cormal and Koola,, saying, "Come with me. We'll walk around the camp and check sentries and positions while we talk. I'm curious about you, Gem."

Gem fell in with them as Cormal nodded. "We've been wondering why she was chasing that crew alone. But there hasn't really been time to talk about it."

She sighed. "Major, I'm not deliberately trying to be mysterious. It's been busy around here. And when I met Cormal and Koola, I was pretty scared until I found out they weren't enemies."

The major nodded. "I understand that. How long had you been tracking the outlaws?"

"Almost a week. At first I thought these two were part of their gang."

Cormal laughed. "She nearly licked Koola and me both, together, mind you. She's one fine fighter. Major."

Gem warmed to the praise. She had seen Cormal in action enough to value his opinion. "I was lucky. Caught them by surprise, mostly," she said.

"But what were you doing there?"

She paused and turned to face the officer. "Looking for my kidnapped son."

The three men looked down at her, their faces sober in the dim light.

"Major, a year ago in the autumn, the Seahawks raided my home village, Dover. They killed my man and took my only son. I was on my way to Portland...to the slave pens... when I came across those raiders on the trail."

Kenteen studied her for a long moment. He shook his head. "Your son was taken, and you set off alone to find him? Did you think you could rescue him alone?"

"I had Merry and Berry. And I got the best training there

is, before I started out. I trained for a year or more with Randor of Dover."

Kenteen's eyes widened. He ran a hand through his snowy hair, then sighed. "Randor! I thought he'd be dead, long ago. He taught you?"

She nodded. "I can hold him at bay all day in a fair fight, if I'm lucky. He always beats me, in the end, but I can take it for hours."

"Even with such training, you have undertaken an enormous task. And even if you find your son, you may find it impossible to break him free." Kenteen ran his finger across the stubble of his chin. He looked thoughtful. Then he grinned. "Remarkable. What can I do to be of assistance?"

Gem stared up at him. "Let me ride with your scouts."

Cormal looked shocked. "Hold on there! We're going after an *army* of raiders, not just a handful. It's no place for you!"

She glanced at him sharply. "I'm talking to the major," she said.

"But Gem...." Cormal sputtered. Koola pulled the tail of his tunic. "Let Small-boots finish," the Macaque hissed into his ear.

Kenteen turned to Gem. "Why?" he asked her.

She drew a deep breath. "Firstly, I have no love for kidnappers and murderers. I'll do what I can to see them wiped out. Secondly, after I help you, then possibly you will help me."

"How?"

"What will you and First Dog do when you finish off Kray and his bunch?"

"Send a report back to Portland."

"You wouldn't object if I rode along with the bunch who takes the report back?"

"Oh, of course. Not at all. Only too glad to help. I'm sure my scouts will welcome your help," he said, holding out his hand. She took it in a firm grip. "Welcome to First Dog, Gem of Dover," he said.

He turned to the others. "Now let's find the quartermaster and the cook. I'm starving to death."

He nodded, arm crooked. Gem parodied his formal gesture in a curtsey. Cormal, still flustered, followed while Koola held back, his wise eyes twinkling.

That night, the camp was hectic, the former captives intoxicated with happiness at being free. The troopers waited on the exhausted women. Sergeant Lanse and Koola took charge of entertaining the children. When stories palled, Koola showed a surprising talent for juggling, keeping strange assortments of pebbles and cups and harness pieces looping in the air for incredible lengths of time. He even juggled knives, sending the bright blades flashing skyward, to land safely each time in his skillful hands and fly upward again.

Kenteen found a chance, while everyone watched the Macaque, to talk with Jace. "I'd like to send you all home at once with a good escort," he told her. "But I'm going into rough country, and I'm outnumbered pretty badly, I suspect. I can't spare a man. Only a good-sized group could be sure of getting all of you back safely."

Jace was matter-of-fact. "Major, we know what you're doing. You're a good man with a big job. Most of us lost kin—some lost all of 'em when the raiders hit us. We've got nothing to rush back to. We don't intend to drag you down, either. We'll tend to the cooking and do anything else we can find to do. We won't complain." She set her thin jaw and looked up with determination.

"We'll be no bother. Most of us have spent our lives wandering through these parts, too. We may be able to guide you same. Anyway, we'll help all we can. You can take us home after you skin that crooked monkey. Is that a deal?"

Kenteen looked carefully at the woman. Washed and fed, she would be a fine-looking woman, though still very thin. Courage shone through her tired features.

Kenteen thought of Gem, then of Jace. Frontier women were a different breed, he thought, putting out his hand. "Madame, it will be our pleasure to have you along."

Jace, unused to such citified courtesies, blushed; she smiled nervously, as she brushed a strand of brown hair away from her face. When Kenteen walked away, her gaze followed him. She had never known a gentleman like that, and she found herself liking the feeling of being close to

100

such a man.

Cormal passed her, moving toward Gem. He nodded approvingly when he saw her getting ready to bed down for the night between her huge pets. The furry beasts would warm away the chill.

"Cormal," Gem said, turning to look up at him.

"Didn't mean to disturb you." He turned away.

She sat up and shook her head. "I'm not ready to sleep yet. Just getting ready."

He shrugged. "I just wanted to apologize far butting in."

"Oh. About riding along with you?"

"Yes. Koola was right. It wasn't my business to interfere. I'm sorry. Okay?"

She smiled. "You were just worried about me. I recognize all the symptoms—my mother does the same. It felt sort of good, actually. Don't bother yourself about it."

There was an awkward moment of silence. She looked into his face, and her expression went serious. Something had almost been said. Something important. But it wasn't time for it to be put into words.

Cormal hunkered dawn and extended his hand. "Friends?"

She shook it enthusiastically. "Friends."

He rose and stretched. "Better rest. We've got a hard ride tomorrow."

She stared into the darkness to the north. "Heading for the mountains?"

"That's the plan. If we can find Kray's camp, we've got 'em for sure." He looked about. "Better turn in myself. Good night."

Gem watched him stride away. Feeling vaguely comforted, she pulled her cape and her blanket about her and snuggled tightly against Merry's furry back.

* * * * * * *

The sun rose into a cloudless sky. The crisp winter air seemed charged with energy. At first light the camp buzzed with activity. Cook-fires dotted the clearing. Hasty breakfasts were prepared and eaten standing, by both troopers and

101

civilians.

Gem found herself hard put to keep Merry and Berry from hunting out the source of the honey-scent that came from the piles of flour-cakes and warmed honey. After rounding up some scraps far them, she joined Koola and Cormal at the major's side, with the troop's four other scouts and the officers.

She pushed between two captains and the lieutenants. Kenteen stood, bare-chested, with a towel about his neck, seemingly impervious to the cold air as he scanned the nearby terrain. She pushed closer to stand with her two friends.

Kenteen saw her and nodded, his eyes continuing to move. "We need to move out as soon as possible. This is indefensible terrain, and I'm not happy to have been here even this long. We'll break camp in fifteen minutes. Captain Roper, take your detachment out first. Dramus, you bring up the rear. Post outriders on each flank. One-mile range unless they have to bring in news or warn of hostiles."

Captain Roper said, "Sir, what about the women and children?"

"Sergeant Lanse and a squad have been detailed to carry them double. They will stay in the center of the column. We've given these people our protection. No harm will come to them as long as any of us are alive. Right?"

The officers looked pleased as they agreed.

"Now for the scouts. Thanks to Cormal and Koola, as well as to Gem, we have proof that we're closing in on the base camp of the raiders. Jace says the mountains are less than a week's journey from here. That's our goal. The raiders said enough within hearing of the captives for us to be pretty sure where they're heading."

An aide handed him his woolen tunic. Kenteen donned it without interrupting the flow of orders. "From now on, scouts range north, as far as they can without losing contact.

"Find the raiders' trail. We still need to know exactly which mountain they're heading for." He set his furry cap on his head and turned to the quartermaster. "I understand, Sergeant Curlon, that provisions are being depleted. Our personal supplies of meal will keep us going for a while, but we need meat. Before getting beyond range, the scouts might kill enough fresh game to carry us for a time." He paused and looked around. "I don't know about you, but I'm getting pretty sick of cornmeal cakes."

There came a chorus of "amen." Travel without their supply wagons had increased speed and mobility, but the diet was less than choice. All tough professionals, they nevertheless enjoyed griping about rations.

When they'd been dismissed, Cormal, Koola, and Gem made for their mounts.

"It will be good to hunt again," Gem said as she mounted Merry. The bearfox danced about as if she agreed.

* * * * * * *

They rode at an easy pace for several hours, alert for signs of either outlaws or game. The surrounding land about them was hilly but fairly open, the trees falling away to show vistas of unspoiled snow, so bright that it almost blinded them.

They forded several creeks, and they found one secluded pond before Gem brought down a large rabbit. As she tied the carcass to her saddle, Cormal said, "There's supposed to be a big lake someplace near here. If we can find it, there should be herds of deer close by."

Encouraged, they pushed on. There had been no sign, so far, of either dogs or humans. For the time being, that suited them. They needed food supplies first.

Then Koola, riding point, topped a hill ahead of them and pulled up his mount. "Lake be there!" he shouted, waving an arm forward.

It was the biggest lake Gem had seen. The water went away into the distance until it was only a misty interface between lake and sky. It reminded her of the sea, for its surface was furrowed into fair-sized waves that washed onto the shore below them.

Koola was pointing. "Look! By shoreline, in trees!"

Cormal squinted in the direction Koola indicated. Shapes moved in the bushes, hard to identify at this distance. Then a huge buck, antlers many-pronged, stepped into full view.

"Snow deer!" Cormal exclaimed.

They were amazed at their luck. The meat of the snow deer was unusually tender, and the hides were valued for their thickness and warmth. The animals were rarely found in winter. They were wily creatures, and their snow-colored coats provided excellent camouflage. Yet here was a fair-sized herd, huddled into a smallish area.

Gem readied her bow. Cormal held up his hand. The others bent forward to listen to his whispered words. "The bearfoxes will force an all-out chase," he began. "The deer have the lake at their backs. If Koola and I charge down from right and left, they'll break up this slope to escape. If Gem is hidden with her pets, she should be able to bring down several." The others quickly agreed.

Cormal and Koola went down the slope at full speed, at angles converging on the herd below. Gem slid from her saddle and led her beasts into a thicket. She looped her quiver over her shoulder in the convenient way Randor had shown her. "Be still!" she hissed at the bearfoxes.

They grumbled softly, but they stood alert and still as she moved away to find her own hiding place. She saw Cormal reach the lake. He pulled Gold around to skirt its edge. The dog barked loudly, and the deer bolted from the grove, moving away from him.

Then Koola was bearing down, his dog-steed yapping wildly. The white beasts panicked and started to scatter. A frightened doe ran into the freezing water at the lake's edge. The buck shook his antlers and started up the slope to the hilltop. A group of does and yearlings followed him.

Gem counted. Almost twenty, she thought. She nocked her first arrow and spoke to her charges. "Quiet...here they come!"

The buck was making huge leaps, higher and higher to clear the deep snow. Gem sighted on the broad chest. He sprang upward; she loosed her arrow. The buck bugled and fell back onto its haunches.

A second beast tried to veer away, but the next arrow caught it in the side. Two does tried to maneuver around the fallen buck. Berry rumbled into motion. He fell upon them and they were dead in seconds.

Now the herd was mad with fear. As animals scattered in all directions, Gem sighted on a third target. She failed to see a young buck bearing down on her right side.

Merry bumped her from behind, sending her sprawling as the enraged buck swung its rack of antlers at her. Merry raked at the beast, but it was going too fast. Her claws caught only air. Now the buck, which was almost as tall as the bearfox, circled cautiously, its antlers held at the ready. Before it could make a move, Gold was behind it, sinking his teeth into one haunch. The buck spun.

In avoiding the rush of the huge deer, the dog almost unseated Cormal. That was all the distraction Merry needed. Before the buck could react, she pounced on its back. Her weight drove it to its knees, and as the buck struggled to rise, the bearfox bit into the powerful neck while her paws were busy at its throat. The buck collapsed into the snow. Merry sniffed at the blood streaming from the carcass.

As Gem dusted snow from herself, Koola rode up. "Small-boots, you okay?"

"Fine, thanks to Merry."

"Good job with arrows. Much meat. Major be happy."

They began gutting their kill. By the time First Dog caught up, they had most of it cleaned. The weariness of the trail vanished from the faces of troopers and civilians alike as they saw the fresh-killed meat.

Jace and the rest took upon themselves the task of cutting up and dividing the kill, passing a share to each platoon. Cook fires blazed up quickly on the shore of the lake. As no one had reported sighting the outlaws, Kenteen agreed to camp long enough to rest and prepare the meat for carrying.

Kenteen bivouacked in a triangular formation, double-picketed on the two landward sides. The lake formed the third side. It was not a bad spot, if defense were necessary. Once the people were busy with their cooking, Koola sought out Gem. "We talk. Something important."

She sat on a log-end beside a fire and looked up at him. He crouched beside her, the rear of his cape ridiculously extended by his long tail. He stared into her eyes.

"I study you. Way you look. Way you move." He indicated the defiant tilt of her head. "Your boy tak'n by Sea-hawks, fall a year ago, yes?"

She nodded, her eyes clouding with pain. "Yes. It seems like a lifetime, now."

"Small-boots, did boy look like you?"

She jerked upright. "What? Why?"

Koola fidgeted. He didn't want to arouse hope that might cause disappointment, but he had a feeling.... "I mean, you his moth'r. Maybe have same-like eyes? Nose like you?"

"A bit. He was blond, like his father, but they told me he looked like me, too. Nel said he had my eyes. What are you getting at?"

Koola took her hand in his small hard fingers. "Small-boots, before Cormal and Koola join soldiers, we live Port-land town. Soon before last winter, Seahawks come there, sell slaves."

Gem's head came up, her forehead furrowing.

"One slave was boy. Yellow hair, yes. But much like you. Big eyes like you. Brave like you. Remind me of you since first we meet. Only now I have time track down what bother me."

"Koola...are you sure?"

The Macaque shrugged. "Maybe so. First time I see you, little voice inside say, 'That like somebody you see 'fore.' Seem like I know you, then all things happ'n, we busy-busy. Now I think of Portland, that boy. Wonder."

"Do you recall what he was wearing?"

Koola grinned. "Not forget anything 'bout that boy. Liked him. Wanted to help. He have on blue smock, brown pants. He have scar over both eyes...like this." Koola sketched a short line above his brows.

Gem's heart skipped a beat.

"When he was three, Little Nel knocked down a hoe from the wall. It put that cut on his head. Oh, Koola, it has to be Nel. It just has to be! Who bought him from the Hawk-ers?"

"Nobody. Cormal and I put all money together. Off'r to buy, make free. Seahawks no take arg'nts for little yellow-hair. They say he strong, brave, too much to be slave. They

106

take him to island to make into Seahawk like them."

Her look of hope was replaced by one of despair. She dropped her head into her hands. Her long tail of hair swung over her shoulder.

Koola tugged at her hand. "He plenty strong. Son of Small-boots...you plenty strong, too. He alive. Koola know, for sure. Get near 'nough. Koola know him. Know we get near. If he be alive, we find him. Koola and Cormal help Gem."

His wizened monkey face wrinkled with his intensity.

Gem smiled, realizing that despair in the face of such unexpected good fortune was foolish. Koola was assuring her that Nel had been alive and well a year ago. He had held his own, even with the Hawkers. He was like his father...and like her, too. Not any of the family ever gave up. She was ashamed of her momentary weakness.

She took Koola's hard little hand. "Somehow, I'll get to Portland. From there I'll find those pirate islands, if I have to learn to be a sailor, too, to do it. Once I find Nel, woe betide anyone who gets in my way."

Even as she spoke, there came a cry from the perimeter of the camp. There were yells; dogs barked hysterically. The noise grew louder, as the pair rose to their feet.

There came a cry from the distance.

"Attack! We're under attack!"

CHAPTER TEN

Captain Slator's fists clenched spasmodically. He stood at attention, trying to conceal his fury, his vicious eyes blank to hide his hatred.

General Tion stood at attention, as he did when disciplining officers, glaring at the over-privileged man. "You are a disgrace not only to your unit and your fellow officers but also to your family. Only that relationship has kept me from asking you to resign your commission on several occasions before this. To beat your serving-wench to a bloody wreck with your fists on the streets of Portland, simply because she failed to black your boots properly, is a matter that cannot be concealed or excused."

Slator was thinking, *I'm the Queen's cousin. He can't talk that way to me!*

Tion went on sternly, "What on earth came over you, Slator? Surely you, of all my officers, should understand the obligations of those in high position to set an example!"

"Sir, it was a matter of discipline....," Slator began.

"Discipline? Are you mad? You beat that girl almost to death in the public square at midday, surrounded by anyone who cared to watch you. In full view of the very ones who are arguing against the prerogatives of the militia within the confines of the town."

"But servants must be kept in their places—"

"A woman at that! You've been a matter of disruption to my command since you entered it. And dammit, Man, you are an embarrassment to me personally. The corps has covered for you more than once." Tion looked at Slator sharply. "Not through affection, I might add. Simply trying to protect itself from our detractors. But now you've put yourself beyond the limits of our patience or our protection. We couldn't pretend this hasn't happened, even if we wanted to."

"Might I remind the General that my cousin would not...."

"Would not what?" roared Tion. He slapped the desktop with both hands.

Slator closed his mouth. Sweat was popping out on his forehead. He hadn't dreamed that there might exist an area in which his kinship with the Queen would not be of help to him.

Tion squared his shoulders and eyed his subordinate. There was contempt in his gaze. "Sir, you are a disgrace. Your fellow officers have said it. Your men cannot say it, but their glances when you pass should leave your back bloody with their contempt.

"You have disrupted the affairs of my command for the last time. As of this moment, you are demoted to the rank of brevet-lieutenant and assigned permanently to barracks duty. Given cause, I will reduce your rank still further."

Disbelief was written on Slator's face. His mouth opened. "But you can't do that!"

"I just did, *Lieutenant* Slator. I suggest that you go before I begin to think myself lenient."

Slator stood, frozen, for an instant. Then, without saluting, he dashed from the room. Before he reached the compound, he had managed to control himself to some extent, though his face was flushed, his eyes blazing, with fury. He checked his stride, then spun and headed off in the opposite direction.

Seething inside, he walked toward the royal residence, which was attached to the farther area of the militia compound. His cousin had always settled his problems for him. Well she knew it might have been him instead of her on the throne of Portland. Perhaps she was grateful. More likely she pitied him. The scar on his face reminded her, inevitably, of the family disturbance that had caused it.

He cracked his heels against the cobbles, turned the comer. Tion was jealous. That was it. Jealous. Incompetent. With only a little imaginative detail, he could make accusations against the general that would look very ugly to his cousin.

She would be easy to sway, he mused as he fingered the scar on his face. He had always been able to manage the Queen. He had used upon her the methods he had learned as a child, setting family members against each other, servants against servants. He had learned to gain what he wanted deviously.

The guard at the gateway stopped him and led him into the foyer at the entrance. The major in charge of the Guard stepped inside and recognized him.

"Wait here," he said. He didn't sound friendly, but he had never been a friend to Captain Slator.

"I have come to see my cousin," Slator barked. The major kept walking, showing no sign that he had heard.

As he waited, the new lieutenant paced the narrow space restlessly. He would make Tion eat his rash words. Maybe he could manage a reduction in rank for the general. A delicious thought. And such poetic justice, as well. His thoughts were interrupted by the return of the major.

"The Queen specifically denies audience to Lieutenant Slator."

Slator felt himself turn pale. General Tion! That old fox had gone straight to her, knowing that he would race to his cousin. He'd told his own version of the incident and turned the Queen against him!

The major continued his set speech. "The Queen admonished Lieutenant Slator to mend his behavior. He will not visit her until such time as observation and report prove that he has changed his character and his manner."

Without waiting for Slator to speak, the major took him firmly by the elbow and hurried him to the gate, where he was ejected into the street with enjoyable force.

Stunned by this reversal of the state of his universe, Slator walked aimlessly, disoriented and furious. Never had he thought to change anything about his life or his behavior. He had no intention of doing so now. Consumed with anger, he walked until he found himself at a seedy pub on the waterfront, where an empty table at the rear beckoned him. He proceeded to drink himself into a stupor.

That drunken state was populated, however, by forms

110

and faces that disturbed him. Kenteen...righteous, insulting, always getting the glory and the praise.

Tion...a toy soldier, full of rigid rules. Rules were all right for the commoners, but for such as Slator they would always be waived. Slator gritted his teeth. A wind-up toy, with no understanding of the needs of a gentleman.

The face of his cousin floated in the mist. Jeering. Condemning him unheard. *He* should have sat on her throne, held the power she used so weakly. If his father had not refused the opportunity of a crown for his only son.... The bitterness of that memory washed over him. The scorn in his father's eyes as he told him of his decision, the rush of hot fury that had sent him at the old man's throat, the terrible agony of the fire on his face...those things he pushed back into the mists, determined not to think of them again.

Instead, his mind churned madly with plans for vengeance. All the smirking grins of his enemies would be wiped away. By what? He would think of something. His superior brain would come up with a suitable plan. It had never failed him. Portland, the Queen, Tion, the people who jeered at him behind his back, all would suffer horribly for this indignity. Power. He would have that. Vengeance, too, would be his.

The plan would come to him, he knew. In a gray fog, he stumbled from the tavern to head for his quarters. In the dusk, the waters of the bay lapped at the breakwater as the tide came in. Guards stalked along the quays. Far out over the misty waters he could see the watch-towers. They were just now lighting their torches against the darkness. High in each lower, he knew, were two human watchmen and one Macaque. He had often supervised the supplying of the lowers and the changing of their duty-rosters. The presence of the monkey-men meant that the harbor was safe from the attack of pirates. Everyone in Portland town knew that, from the harbormaster to the dumbest whore on the waterfront.

Slator stared at the towers, fascinated. Something nagged at his mind. The security of the entire town lay in the hands of those watchmen. With the suddenness of a lightning-bolt the answer came to him. His revenge. In one swoop he could savage Tion, humble the Queen, and spite the town, which had gossiped about him, passed scandal and rumor about him from tongue to tongue, ever since he was fourteen. With the help of...yes, he might even be the next ruler of Portland, a very different ruler, if all went well.

If he had the daring, it was within his reach. A smile, cruel as the snarl of a wolf, split his sallow face. Suddenly sober. Slator ran toward the compound. He felt better than he had felt all day.

* * * * * * *

Corporal Deran was very busy. His fingers fumbled at the kitchen maid's blouse with clumsy eagerness. Her giggles made her figure bounce deliciously. Deran had been waiting impatiently for this moment ever since the mess sergeant had hired the wench.

The shed door burst open. Captain Slator stood over him. Deran felt his heart jump almost through its prison of ribs and skin. The man looked crazy.

"Deran! I need you! Come!"

The girl pulled away and caught her blouse together at the neck. Slator didn't notice her, it seemed, even when she fled past him.

"Back to the kitchen!" Deran snapped. The command was unnecessary. She was gone.

Slator closed the door. The corporal swallowed. The man's eyes were always odd, but now they seemed almost glazed. Who knew what the devil he was up to now? "Cap'n...," he began.

"Shut up! Listen to me!"

"Yessir!"

Slator opened the door a crack and peeped out. Then he closed it and bent over Deran, who hadn't dared to move. "I am now a lieutenant. Remember that. What I am about to say is between you and me only. Is that clear?"

"Yessir, Cap'n. I mean Lieutenant!"

"Keep your voice down!"

"Yessir." Deran could feel his teeth beginning to chatter.

"I need information. Only you, of all the men I know, can provide it. I have heard that your cousin went with the Seahawks. Is that true? Is he still with them?"

Deran felt his stomach turn queasy. He had felt the kiss of Slator's whip. It had infected him with a terrible fear. "He is, sir."

"I want an interview with their leader."

"Sir?" Deran couldn't believe what he was hearing. Fear chilled his skin.

"I want," Slator said with dangerous precision, "to talk with the captain of the Seahawks. Do you understand me? Can you arrange that?"

Deran shuddered. "Not personally. But I can get word to my cousin. He may be able...but...pardon, sir, but...why?"

Slator pulled the young man to his feet. One arm went about his shoulders, and Deran shrank from the contact.

"Because I want to get out to Blood Island. You will help me to get there."

"Yessir," said Deran, through chattering teeth. He was terrified...but what could he do?

CHAPTER ELEVEN

The outlaws' night raid on the lakeside camp was only the first of many. Hit and run assaults were launched against Kenteen's troops at unanticipated intervals, in unsuspicious places. More than one sentry fell to arrows from hidden bows. And by the time the troopers were roused from their rest to charge off into the night, the marauders were gone. It was just as frustrating trying to move by day.

A second attack came several days later, just before dawn. Cook fires were being stoked. Everyone was groggy with sleep. Gem had washed her face in the brook near the camp when a group of shouting dog-riders burst from the forest, swords unsheathed. Another harassment attack, she knew, for there were few dogs and men. She didn't pause to stare. She grabbed her blade and yelled to Merry and Berry as she ran toward the spot where they were now engaged with sleepy troopers.

Two of the soldiers lay dead. One outlaw turned to meet her, as she ran up. She dove beneath his thrust to bury her point in his leg. He cursed, trying to catch her on the back-swing, while controlling his plunging dog at the same time. She parried the clumsy blow and almost unseated him. While he was off-balance, she struck upward, felt the brief resistance of a rib, then the slip of the blade into his heart.

As she tugged it free, her two beasts lumbered up, panting and growling. The outlaws' dogs shrieked with terror, struggling against the reins at the sight and smell of the bear-foxes. Their riders didn't try to hold them. Having hit the camp hard enough to disrupt it, they departed the scene as speedily as they had arrived. Gem vaulted onto Berry's back to follow.

Cormal, running hard, shouted, "Wait for me!"

The outlaws were moving fast. She pointed to the other bearfox. "No time to get Gold. Ride Merry!"

He stared at the brown-furred animal. It snarled and grumbled deep in its throat but offered no threat. Cormal hesitated, but Gem was already out of sight. Berry was faster than anyone would suspect. Cormal grabbed a handful of fur and sprang onto Merry's back. The beast roared and set off after its mate.

As they crashed through the pine grove in pursuit of Gem, he forgot the monster he was riding. The prey was not far ahead. He could hear the yapping of the dogs. Dog-riders had an advantage in the thick growth. Less bulky than the bearfoxes, the animals slid through more easily. Before long, however, they found themselves in old forest that had known storms and lightning-fires. Tangles of brush and deadfall impeded the dogs, now, while the heavier bearfoxes crushed it down and trampled over it.

With their pursuers rapidly gaining, the raiders split up, each riding off into a different direction. Berry was closing in on the heels of a shaggy-coated German Shepherd. The dog, distracted by the bearfox's scent, tried to peer back over its shoulder and ran full-tilt into an oak. Berry lunged, carrying the lighter animal down beneath his weight.

The rider, trapped between his mount and Berry's claws, squirmed, trying to clear his sword. Gem gave a signal. Berry reared back, as steel flashed very near his throat. The bearfox flicked a paw, and the outlaw's head went spinning.

From the left, another raider broke through the undergrowth. His blade was aimed for Gem's back. Berry, still entangled with the fallen dog, couldn't maneuver. Gem twisted in the saddle to meet the new charge.

There came a whoop, and bushes were trampled to splinters. Cormal and Merry, now fully in a killing rage, roared up beside the startled dog and its rider. Cormal dove over Merry's neck onto the outlaw's back. Both sprawled onto the snow. Merry turned her attention to the now-riderless dog.

Gem, still trying to disentangle Berry, tried to see what was happening, but Merry was in the way. All she could see

115

was four human legs, twining and untwining in a death-struggle. The legs spasmed together. One pair went still. Gem held her breath until Cormal's face emerged.

He wiped his knife blade down his trouser-leg. The other dog had fled from Merry, and its horrified yelps *were* dying into the distance.

Gem said, "You ride a mean bearfox, my friend."

Cormal grinned. "Merry is a fine mount. But don't tell Gold I said that."

She stared after the retreating dog. "Should we hunt the rest of them?"

"I think not. They're long gone by now anyway. Best we get back to see if we can help. The major isn't going to be happy."

He wasn't. And he grew no happier as the days passed.

Quick, deadly raids kept his nerve-ridden men and dogs sleepless. The weather changed for the worse, too, with violent storms that rolled out of the mountains to stop them in their slow pursuit, sometimes for days.

Kenteen was too bright to try battling both the weather and Kray. As they approached the base of the mountain range, finally, he set the men to building a semi-permanent fortress-like camp. Working in the stinging snow, the men felled trees and put up four crude shelters on the lee *of the* hill that faced the first mountain slope.

The shelters were set in a hollow square, which provided a secure place for dogs. From the top of the headquarters building, Kenteen had an open view of the surrounding country on the forested side. It was a strategically sound outpost.

Once his people were secure, he sent out patrols and scouts, whose objective was to locate the raiders' base camp. In such weather, it was hard duty. The rescued women, feeling for the men subjected to such weather, put in long hours making the shelters warm and comfortable. None of the troopers, including Kenteen, failed to appreciate their efforts.

Kenteen was no armchair officer. He rode with his patrol every day. Each time he returned to find warm food, hot drink, warmed furs and blankets to thaw out his frozen body, his admiration for Jace grew.

A natural leader, she had taken charge of the women and children. She scrounged and finagled and managed to accomplish things the officer would have thought impossible, given the circumstances. And she kept the civilians quiet and busy.

One morning, ranging far on a small patrol, Kenteen and Cormal discovered their enemies' newest strategy.

The sky had cleared. Only a bit of snow still fell, moving lightly on the breeze. Spirits had risen a bit, when Cormal came racing up.

"What's amiss. Cormal?" the officer asked.

"Up ahead, Major," Cormal said. He looked sick. "You should see it yourself. It's...well, just come, Sir."

Kenteen kicked his dog into motion and rode after the scout into a patch of trees. Beyond a small hill they came into a clearing where the snow was trampled. It had been visited very recently by a large body of men and dogs.

"Raiders?" he asked.

Cormal crossed the open space to a copse laced with fronds of dark green ivy. A gigantic birch loomed over the thicket. Cormal pointed upward, wordless.

Kenteen halted his dog, shading his eyes to see the dark thing hanging in the birch. It swung in the light breeze. His eyes widened. He clenched his teeth.

That had been a man.

Kenteen had seen atrocities before. Hawker raids. Battles with other outlaws had shown him the dark side of humanity that many had never experienced. Yet he had never seen a man butchered in this way.

The body hung from the neck, its limbs and testicles removed. The tongue, swollen and black, protruded from the mouth amid splinters of teeth. The entire thing was black with dried blood. A madman had supervised the torment of this unfortunate man.

"They left us a message, "said Cormal.

Kenteen drew a deep breath. "Do you see his arms and legs any place?"

"Probably fed 'em to the dogs. From the...stuff...on the ground, I'd say they cut him up lying there, then they hung him."

"You think he was still alive...when they did this?"

"I'd guess so, sir. I think this is our missing trooper. Can't swear to it, but it could be."

Kenteen had avoided looking into the terrible face. Now he glanced up at it. He tried to fit those dark, swollen features into his memory of the open face of Private Feldon, who'd never come back from patrol.

They had thought he had been lost in a blinding snowstorm and frozen to death. Now Kenteen wished that had been the case. It would have been far better than this inhuman treatment.

"Cut him down, Cormal. Please."

Without a word, the scout climbed into the branches and cut the rope. He lowered the body gently to the ground, shinnying down after it.

Kenteen had already spread his own cloak over the pitiful remnant. It tore at him to lose men. And this sort of loss filled him with pain and fury.

"Give a hand, will you, Cormal? We can put him on my own mount."

Together they lifted the corpse across the saddle. The major's Irish Setter pranced nervously as they worked. Kenteen caressed her, spoke softly to her, and calmed her to stand. When the bundle was secured, Kenteen mounted to sit behind the grisly burden.

When they reached the camp, Kenteen arranged a military funeral, though they could not bury the man in the frozen ground. A cairn of stones formed his grave. When the ritual was done, the words spoken over the grave, Kenteen turned to his people. "I want to speak to every one of you, soldier and civilian, man and woman and child." He looked about, finding nothing but sober and attentive faces.

"Kray thinks that by torturing our comrade, he will weaken us, make us afraid, send us scurrying home. You have looked upon our dead. What do you say?"

A great shout rose on the frozen air. "NO!!!"

He smiled grimly. "We are not the cowardly sort he supposes us to be. When he cuts one, we all bleed. When they butcher one of ours, we all know his pain. But it makes us strong, not weak. It provides a burning incentive to go

118

forward and to avenge our own. It does not make us fearful."

"No!" came the shout again. The distant peaks seemed to ring with it.

"We will avenge our brother. We swear it by his blood!" Kenteen boomed.

"By the blood of the dead!" came the cry.

Hundreds of blades cleared their sheaths. Hundreds of voices sounded together.

Gem, standing beside Cormal shouted too.

A week later, she disappeared.

CHAPTER TWELVE

The sea played havoc with his stomach, Slator found. Gripping the side of the small skiff, he tried to ignore the insults of the two Hawkers who manned the craft, as well as his own rising nausea.. He glanced up. It was midday. He felt as if he'd been on the icy ocean for days, instead of the hours since midnight. He wondered how much longer he could last, if Blood Island didn't come into view soon.

He also wondered now why he had been so anxious to make the trip. It had taken Deran several weeks to make contact with his kin, and for them to arrange a meeting. He had been on tenterhooks all the while.

Remembering that midnight trek to a deserted cove, where he and Deran had flashed a lantern toward the sea in a coded pattern, the answer after a long delay, and the appearance of the skiff, he tried to revive the feeling of excitement and anticipation of vengeance he had felt. Instead he almost groaned, though he managed to stifle it. The one-masted craft was equipped with a square sail of thick brown canvas. It bellied outward, propelling them quickly but very roughly as they tacked over the swell.

Slator's dinner had gone overboard soon after they cleared the headland. That had amused the Hawkers immensely. It had been a blow to Slator's self-esteem to show such weakness, but there had been nothing to do but upchuck.

He raged at the superior grins of these pirates. He managed to hold his fury in check, but he longed to slice the grins from their faces. Ignorant of boats and oceans and sailing, he could do nothing now. Also, he needed to persuade the leader of the Hawkers of the practicality of his scheme.

Slicing up his sea pilots would not further his cause, he knew. The mariners could continue to grin and chuckle stupidly...for now.

Gulls overhead gave the first indication that they were approaching an island. Slator straightened to peer ahead. Gray dots on the horizon had to be cliffs. Moment by moment, the distant vision took on solidity, distinct outlines. The trip was almost over. He refused to think of his return across the choppy winter sea. One torture at a time was enough.

They passed two stony bars to reach the harbor. Massive cliffs rose, pale and wind-worn, from the sea. Notched into their bases was a fair anchorage, protected from wind from any quarter and invisible from any distance at sea.

As the seamen lowered and lashed the sail, readying for the entry, Slator felt his heart finally rise from his stomach with excitement. If his proposal found favor with these pirates....and if his plot worked out...he would *rule* in Portland, as he should have been doing all along. His arrogant cousin and her ridiculous General Tion would suffer fates worthy of those who set themselves against Augustus Slator!

* * * * * * *

Something unusual was taking place. Nel sensed it. He had been detailed to serve in the captain's hall. He moved from kitchen to tables with his serving tray filled with tankards of ale and dishes of steaming food. This was not normal mealtime chaos, he realized.

When he and the others were in the Hall, Bolton had spoken sternly. "You'll be serving important folk. You'd best be cautious about making mistakes...today. Cap'n Jacker won't look kindly on the boy who fouls an anchor."

Even Dida had been caught by an ear. "Leave the lad be, you hear?" he'd warned her harshly. "Your Pa says that you spill so much as a mug of ale, trying to rankle Nel, he'll have the skin off your bones."

That had astonished Dida...even frightened her. It seemed. Although she had nodded, Nel caught a dangerous sparkle in her eyes. He prayed that for once she would be wise enough to listen to someone. Not that she would!

The doors opened wide to let Jacker enter, leading all his captains from all the other Hawker isles. Rarely did they congregate in one place for very long. Nel ignored the clamor of noise, the smell of unwashed pirates, hot food, and alcohol, so busy were his eyes and ears.

The plates of cod and roast game and vegetables were being filled already when Tarl arrived. With him were two others and a narrow-faced stranger with the meanest eyes Nel had ever seen. As the stranger, who wore a militia uniform, took his place at Jacker's table, a cold lump formed in Nel's stomach. Something bad was afoot.

Between trips to the kitchens and the ale-room, he watched and listened. A word here and a word there gave him a notion of who the man was. But why had he come to Blood Island?

* * * * * * *

Jacker wiped ale-foam from his red beard. He kept looking at Slator...the man had talked without pause through the meal, neglecting his food. The plan he was proposing was wild, even for a Hawker. Jacker belched deeply, then he turned to speak to Slator.

"Look here, Slator. You claim to be able to get rid of the monkey-people in the towers. Right?"

"Yes, I can. It will be no problem to poison their water supply before the night watch goes on duty."

"I can see that. But don't all the Macaques have that second sight?"

"Why...yes. But I don't under—"

"Then what's to stop the others, not those in the tower, but the ones in town, from sensing that we're coming? Even if all the guards be dead?"

Slator smiled, feeling superior. He'd planned carefully and was ready for the question. "In two moons, Portland will hold its Vernal Equinox. Everyone will get drunk, stay that way for days." He chuckled grimly.

"Even if some of the Macaque are sober enough to sense your approach, they'll probably not be certain of it. And if they try to tell anyone, nobody will be sober enough to believe them or to do anything about it if they did. But the Vernal Equinox will be the only time when that will be true. Any time else, it won't work at all. That is why it's important for you to plan the attack now."

"Mmmm," Jacker mused. "The garrison will be at strength?"

"It has been for two winters. The high staff ordered Dog into the wilderness last year to establish new outposts and to secure the route to the Canadas. They won't be back for a long while yet."

Slator felt a strange and sudden uncertainty. Why hadn't the red-bearded pirate leaped at the chance he offered? Why was he sitting there, looking thoughtful. Looking doubtful?

Slator leaned across the table and added emphatically, "The other company is on border patrol. The troop is never full force, not inside the wall."

"It seems a good plan to me," said Tarl, as his leader made no effort to answer.   .

Jacker turned a somber gaze toward Tarl. "I'll make up me own mind," he said. His tone was not cordial.

Slator set down his tankard a bit too hard. "But Captain...Portland is a plum, waiting to drop into your hand!" Tarl nodded agreement, his eyes alight with enthusiasm.

Jack settled back into his chair. "I know too well the rewards of such a venture, if it be successful. But have you given any thought to the grief that might befall us should your plan go sour?"

"Sour?" Slator's voice cracked, but he steadied his nerves. "When I have it all laid out for you? It cannot possibly fail!"

Jacker fixed him with a cold eye. "Don't bluff a Seahawk, Slator. No plan is foolproof. Every raid is a risk, and this one hangs upon your word alone. If you should fail...or betray us...we'd be in for it. Do you expect me to fall in with your plotting like a first-voyage hand? We've lived this long and remained this snug by being cautious when it was warranted. Not by swallowing any bait thrown in our way, eh, men?" He looked from man to man.

Now the faces of the Hawkers, which had been flushed

with eagerness, turned skeptical.

"Listen to me," Slator said, trying to control the panic in his voice, "I can realize the dangers...."

"Can ye, now?" Jack interrupted him. "Maybe ye didn't know that I've sailed into Portland harbor under slave-truce many's the time. I've seen those catapults standing around the bay like so many engines of death. There are enough to sink our fleet many times over, if we should get caught short there."

"But I promise you, the entry will be a complete surprise. You'll be docked and your crews in the town, before anyone can suspect it. That's my job, and I know well how to do it."

Bolton spoke for the first time. "It's a bit much, having to rely so completely on a single man."

Tarl, dizzied by the prospect of loot, so many slaves for the taking, stood unsteadily. "Are we Hawkers or a bunch of old ladies? With this single raid, we'll all be rich as kings!"

"Or cold as dead bait," Bolton roared. "Cap'n, Tarl and his hotheads think with their purses, not their brains."

"Enough!" Jacker crashed his empty tankard to the floor. He heaved a bowl of dried berries after it. The room went silent and still.

Slator clenched his hands in his lap. He had to loose them deliberately from that death-grip.

"We've listened to this man's plans. There are good and bad points. All of us have yearned for Portland like a babe for its mammy's milk, but it's always been beyond reach. The militia and the monkey-folk have seen to that, but Slator says he can take care of such things. Maybe he can. Maybe he can't. It's we Hawkers who'll have to put our necks into the noose to prove it. There's a good chance that such a big raid could go wrong. If it should, few will live to tell the tale, few will come home to Blood Island."

Jack took another tankard from a tray carried by an awe-struck lad and took a long pull. Belching, he thumped it down. "It seems to me we have to think on this plan long while before we put trust in it."

Slator, red with fury, leaped to his feet. "But you can't do that! All will be lost if you don't move now!"

The red beard jerked. "Look, Slator, this is my island. I make decisions here. We have two full moons to decide, isn't that what you said?"

"Yes...but...."

"No buts. Go back to Portland. Calm yourself down. When I've decided to answer you, I'll send for you. Is that clear?"

Slator bit his tongue. He wanted to shout, to scream, to foam with fury. These were cowards, not the bloodthirsty pirates he had always thought! But he controlled his reaction and made his voice sound calm. "Very well. I will await your reply. But I hope that you're not about to make a very big mistake."

"Mistake or no, it's mine and none of yours."

The audience was at an end. Tarl and several others rose. Slator knew his time was over. More talk would be futile. He followed Jacker and his group from the hall.

Those left resumed eating and drinking. Jacker motioned for Bolton to move nearer. The one-legged man slipped across his bench to hear. Jacker put his head near the other man's and spoke quietly. "What do you think of this, Bolton? This Slator...how do you read him?"

"I don't like him a bit, Cap'n. He has his own fish to fry, I think. He's thinking to use us."

"Aye, so I figured it."

"He's a traitor to his own folk. Why should he be faithful to us, once he gets what he wants? Don't trust him, Cap, I say."

Jack leaned back. "Aye, Bolton. We think alike. Slator is a shark. And none knows a shark like a seafaring man."

* * * * * * *

The sun was sinking as the party neared the dock. Slator's spirits were low. He had failed to arrive at a firm deal with Jacker. And now he faced another bout of seasickness. Something inside told him that Jacker had found some fatal flaw in the plan. The whole thing had been for naught.

As two seamen readied the skiff, Tarl came up to Slator and touched his elbow. "I'd like a word with you, alone."

125

Slator looked at Tarl, then at his fellows. He let Tarl guide him to the end of the pier.

"Don't let Jacker discourage you. We're not all old and cautious. There's some..."—He slid his gaze sideways, and Slator shivered at his expression—"...think as Jacker has outlived his time."

Slator narrowed his eyes. New hope surged inside him.

"You think it might be simpler if we two dealt together? Without troubling the old man any more?"

The captain grinned. "Exactly. My friends and I are worried about the Jacker's health. We think he won't be around too much longer. You understand?" He extended his hand.

Slator took it and replied, "I do. You will not regret your...vision."

Tarl frowned. "Go back to Portland and wait. Once we have things in hand, we'll send word."

"And we can work out details later."

"Yes. That's a raid we'll not be denied. Have a good trip. We'll meet again."

Slator turned toward the waiting boat. The sooner the better, he thought.

CHAPTER THIRTEEN

In the northern woods, the days were growing longer. The older troopers of First Dog could smell and feel the subtle change in the crisp air. They knew that rain squalls would soon replace the snow; a gradual warming would signal spring. Except for Cormal, all were in good spirits.

He was worried about Gem. She had vanished ten days before, while on a scouting expedition. Though the troop had searched thoroughly, no trace had been found of her or of Merry and Berry.

He hadn't worried for several days, for it wasn't unusual for a lone scout to pursue some promising traces for as long as a week. But this was different. Scouts usually left marks on trees, signals along the trail. There had been none that anyone could find. He had wanted Kenteen to institute a search after less than a week, but the officer had sensibly refused.

He had withdrawn into a gloomy mood. Even Koola didn't approach him often.

Then Kenteen, too, had become anxious when the tenth day had passed. When the search parties found no sign, he had given orders that every patrol should keep close watch for the missing scout and her beasts.

Six more days went by. Cormal began riding out after dark, weary though he was after a day in the saddle. That was reckless, and the officers frowned upon it, but the men secretly cheered him on. Koola begged Kenteen to order Cormal to rest at night, and Kenteen agreed to speak with him unofficially.

Cormal shook his head. "As long as she's out there, I've got to look," he said. "Sorry, sir, but I've got to go."

127

The major shook his head as he watched the scout draw away into the darkness. If he had ordered him to stay in camp, Cormal would have gone anyway, he knew. Then he would have had to punish him. He knew how worried the man was...he felt the same himself.

Back in his quarters, he flung off his cloak. *Jace* frowned as she put a bowl of stew on his rough-hewn table. "Couldn't stop him? Some are too stubborn for their own good, Major," she said.

He sighed. "If something happens to him, too, it will be my fault."

She gave a whisk of the ladle. "He'd have gone anyway, no matter what you told him. Gem has a grip on him. No order will prevent him from searching."

"But there's no room for that sort of thing on a campaign."

"Nonsense! When any pair can find some peace and comfort in each other, it's a blessed miracle. Might as well try to stop the rain and the wind. It's a force of nature, Major."

He stared at her. She had never spoken so intensely before. Her face, now less thin than it had been, was rosy with determination.

"Now, I wasn't condemning romance. That has its time and place, all proper and in order."

Jace laughed, filled her own bowl, and set it beside his. She wiped her hands on her skirt. "People are never proper and in order," she said.

Instead of sitting down, she came up to him and raised her arms. She pulled his head down and kissed him firmly on the lips. He started, surprised, but she held him tightly. He felt his blood warming at her touch. When she stepped back at last, he was flushed and speechless.

She smiled slightly but said nothing and turned to their supper. After a bit, she chuckled softly. "Major, you are an excellent soldier, but there are a lot of things you still need to learn."

* * * * * * *

Koola was on his way back to barracks from the latrine when Cormal came through the front gate. As the Macaque started toward his friend, he realized that the man was sitting on his dog oddly. As Gold approached, he saw that Cormal was jerking and swaying, literally asleep in the saddle.

"Cormal!" Koola shouted.

The scout shook his head. His eyes opened. "Koola? what're you doin' out here?"

"You idiot! You back in camp!"

"Huh?" When Cormal turned to stare about him, he lost his balance and slid off Gold. Koola was under him to break the fall, and the weight of the scout carried them both to the ground.

"The dog has more sense!" Koola grunted, but his friend was asleep again.

As a pair of troopers carried the snoring man away to his barracks, Koola stared away toward the mountains. "Small-boots," he mourned. "Will see again? Ever?" in his own tongue, the Macaque made a little prayer to his own inscrutable gods. Somehow, it comforted him as he turned back toward the camp.

* * * * * * *

Deep in the mountains, Gem was moving rapidly, riding Berry and closely followed by Merry. They had been following this trail for days, and they'd taken up the tracking as soon as there was light to see. In two weeks, they had come from the foothills into the heart of the mountain range. There was no turning back, for this was a group of dog-riders who seemed to be headed, at speed, straight for some familiar goal.

Gem knew that her companions, back in camp, would be frantic. Yet she knew she was on the heels of a band of riders who were headed home. She could do nothing but follow. The signs she left on the trail were far beyond any place the patrols would come, she understood quite well. And if she stopped her pursuit to return for help, any shower of rain or flurry of snow would wipe out the traces she followed.

There was also a dilemma—every day the tracks were

129

fresher, as were the dogs' droppings. She was closing on her quarry. Proceeding into unknown territory alone was not wise, but there was no way for her to summon help. This was the clearest sign yet of Kray's elusive camp. She could hear the yapping of dogs far ahead. No, she could not abandon the chase now.

She pulled Berry to a halt, cautioning both animals to be silent. She eased through the trees and looked across a shallow valley. A file of riders was moving up a small rise. There were six mounted dogs, traveling at an easy pace. They seemed to have no suspicion that they were being followed. She moved into higher country, leaving the lower ranges behind. Her quarry rode on after darkness fell. Only then did the raiders make camp.

Gem made a cold camp at a considerable distance, blessing Sergeant Lanse's order that required every trooper to carry double rations when going on scout. From her supply of jerky and cold biscuit, she fed herself and her companions. She could only hope that her journey would not be so long that she ran out of supplies.

Huddling at last between the bearfoxes, she slept deeply. But she woke at first light. When the raiders moved, before sunrise, Gem was behind them. The exhilaration of the hunt had subsided into boredom, but she kept doggedly on the track.

One morning the pace of those she followed seemed to quicken. The group, glimpsed from the side of a mountain, seemed to be excited and full of nervous energy. Gem dropped farther back to let them outdistance her. She knew their direction.

There had to be a heavy guard around Kray's encampment. She didn't want to stumble into any pickets who might range far out, and she knew the bearfoxes' acute senses, now that they had seen and scented their prey, could direct her with fair accuracy, if she needed to approach again. By midday the slope they'd been climbing leveled out a bit. Far ahead there was a noise...voices of men and dogs. The men she was following must have reached their destination.

She dismounted to edge forward on foot. The sparse wood concealing her ended at a rocky clearing. She could see that she was halfway up a mountain, whose peak was hidden in clouds. She slipped behind a boulder and slowly rose to peer over it.

Beyond a clearing, a foaming creek of winter runoff cut its way through a gap in the rock. Beyond it, hidden by a screen of trees and bushes, was the enemy camp. She had found it!

She recorded every detail in her memory. The entry was a cavern hollowed into the face of the mountain. Smaller caves dotted the rock face higher up. Hundreds of people, it seemed to her, were moving in the clearing before the cave-mouth and in and out of the tunnel itself. Children were scampering about. She thought she could see flickers in the black depths of the mountain that must be fires. At one side of the cliff holding the cave was a shelter for dogs or supplies. On the other side were open pens used to hold the animals in summer. A number of them now milled about there... dogs of every sort.

The patrol she had followed was making its way up the farther bank of the creek, surrounded by many welcoming people. Among them was a figure in a gray cloak, whom no one jostled. It was short, and it walked with the strange gait of a Macaque.

Kray!

His camp was enormous. The major's men would find it hard to take, she knew, defended as it was by the stone of the mountain itself. But if she could return safely to the troop, she might give Kenteen the edge he needed. She prepared to move...but a motion off to her left froze her again into stillness. A man, crouched in the shadow of another boulder, was watching the festivities, failing, for the moment, in his sentry duty. She knew there would be more.

Before moving, she picked out two more on her side of the stream and at least another pair positioned on the mountainside above the cavern. Kray knew how to set a guard.

She slid backward, shielded by the stone, into a thicket. When she got back to the bearfoxes, she whispered to Berry, "Easy. Slowly. Quietly." But she knew they always moved with stealth through the forest.

They eased back along the track until they were over the

shoulder of the mountain. Then she headed directly across country, toward Kenteen's winter camp. She took the mountainside in hairpin turns, hoping to cross the rushing creek well south of the outlaw stronghold. In a few hours they found the icy flow barring their progress. She decided to fill her water bags there, to save time later. She took them downslope to the slabs of stone edging the creek. Berry and Merry waded into the shallows below her to quench their thirst.

She lifted the filled bags to her shoulder and carried them to a fallen log to reposition them. As she followed them, she heard a growl...almost at her back. She turned to meet the danger as a flash of blue-black and a terrible set of shining fangs caromed into her. There was sudden pain in her left shoulder. She was down, rolling, banging against stones. A grumbling roar filled her ears, and she screamed.

The rock-cat backed away for an instant, startled. She could see the long-muscled body, the tremendous size, the razor-sharp fangs. There were the two bone knobs the males always sprouted at their temples. Staring into the blood-red eyes, Gem willed herself to move.

She rolled again, desperately, trying to draw her blade. When she came to rest against a set of huge roots, she had her sword out, but the hurtling rock-cat bowled her over again. A knob caught her at the base of her neck. The beast was holding her with its forelegs, ripping at her heavy clothing with its hind claws. She fought insanely. To pause was to die.

The blade made contact for a second. Then the rock-cat cried shrilly and moved away from her, propelled by a furry body hitting it from one side. Berry. The two rolled, biting and clawing, while Gem struggled to stand. Merry was there, nudging at her, supporting her. She clung to the warm fur as she watched the terrible battle.

The beasts were well-matched in ferocity, though the rock-cat was much larger. Both were covered with blood by the time the rock-cat backed away, laid back its ears, and charged. Berry reared, clawed pads waiting. They met full-on. Fangs and claws tore into Berry's body, but his own claws were working on the cat, as well. They parted again.

132

This lime Berry slumped back onto his haunches.

The cat was moving, but its front legs buckled beneath its weight. Berry was still worse off...he could barely remain upright. Gem knew he would perish when the rock-cat hit him again, if she didn't do something instantly.

Holding onto Merry's fur, she shouted into the creature's ear, "Kill, Merry! Now!" She loosed her grip.

Merry lunged forward, fresh, eager to avenge her sibling. The rock-cat turned to meet her, but Berry's efforts had weakened it. It managed one swipe of its claws. Then Merry caught his head between her paws. She pulled away flesh and skin. The cat convulsed, came up, dug claws into Merry, bringing its neck into range of her teeth. The bearfox snapped into the exposed throat. With a jerk, her fangs almost tore the head free of the neck. The bearfox shook the beast twice, then let the body fall, nudging it to make sure it was dead.

Satisfied, she went to Berry. Licking his wounds, she made soft little sounds of grief deep in her throat. He turned himself to let her reach the worst of his gashes. Now Gem thought to check herself over. Her neck wound was deep, the shoulder was painful but not dangerous. The other cuts were minor. She would be fine if she could stop the bleeding from her neck. Bruises would show up for days, but they would be nothing to worry about.

She ripped cloth from her shirt, wet it in the icy water, and pressed it against her neck. Then she turned to the animals. She felt dizzy, but she took deep, slow breaths, controlling it. She couldn't let herself go into shock.

She knew that she was in trouble. She was still many miles from the troop, in a strange forest, with enemies just beyond the ridge, with night coming...She had to find shelter—for Berry and for herself. They couldn't survive a night in the cold, she knew.

She touched his furry head. "Come. Berry. We'll find a place to bed down." He looked at her, his eyes questioning. One was clotted with blood and torn flesh. He was dripping blood from all over his body. "Please, boy. Get up. For Merry. For me. Please?"

He surged forward slowly onto his forepaws. She

pushed from behind, to help him. At last he stood, wobbly, insecure, on his own legs. She patted him, motioning for Merry to check out the terrain up the slope. As they started, Gem recalled the water bags. She retrieved them, though the straps cut into her wounds. When Merry returned, she tied them onto her saddle and began climbing.

She could, of course, have ridden Merry, but Berry needed her support as he struggled up the slope. She walked beside him to find a safe spot in which to tend his wounds. She had a hard time keeping him moving. Long after dark, they found a little cave in the side of a projecting bluff.

Once Merry checked it out for present tenants, Gem urged Berry into it. He collapsed into a furry heap. Merry began licking his wounds instantly.

Gem slid down the wall of the cave. In the darkness she could hear the soft lapping of the bearfox's tongue. From time to time, Berry whimpered quietly. Too weary to think, Gem allowed herself to sink into unconsciousness.

* * * * * * *

Screams in the night woke Nel. Shrieks...yells...curses. The racket filling the air tugged him out of sleep. Disoriented, he lay still on his hard cot, curled close beneath a rough woolen blanket. He tried to sort sense from the noise. People were running over the stony paths. There were crashes and splinterings, as if doors were being bashed in. Things broke. Steel clashed against steel.

He pulled on clothing and boots. The hide shirt that had been a gift from Bolton made him wonder what his teacher was doing. He lit a candle and moved toward the old pirate's bed. Bolton was stirring, not yet awake. He had been drunk when he came home, very late. Nel had put him to bed, expecting that he would sleep the clock around. But now he was waking.

"Whaz alla ruckus?" Bolton mumbled, feeling for his peg leg. Nel brought it and helped him buckle it on. The old man stared up at the boy questioningly.

"They're fighting out there," said Nel, opening the door a crack. Bolton stumped up behind him, and they both stared out at the moonlit plaza.

Dark shapes moved. Shouting, swords flashing and clanging. Nel could see Jacker's shape, his hair and beard red even in the moonlight. About him a group clustered in front of the Hall. They fought madly, and their attackers fell, groaning, to the stony paving. The glare of the attackers' torches made the scene hellish—blood was redder than it seemed in daylight; the eyes of the dead gleamed malevolently. A corpse lay almost before Bolton's door, and Nel kept his gaze resolutely away from the pallid face, the half-opened eyes.

He looked, instead, at Jacker's hard-pressed defenders. More were now dead than alive, lying among those they had killed. Even as he watched, Jack himself went down, his flaming hair quenched at last in dark blood. The two who had stood at his back followed at once, overwhelmed by their opponents. In an instant, the mutineers claimed victory, holding their blazing torches high over the carnage.

Behind Nel, Bolton groaned. The boy knew that a great part of the old man's life seemed ended with the fall of his leader. The one-legged man stared wildly about, seemingly addled with the terrible change in his life, as well as the drink of the night before.

"What's happened?" he asked, as if he had not seen Jacker fall. "What's goin' on? Tell me, boy!"

"Something bad. You saw it," said Nel. "We'd better go...they're dangerous."

"You follow my lead," said Bolton, rousing himself from his shock. He stumped into the street.

The place was full of people, and more were being roused from their homes. Sleepy men, women, and children were herded together before the doors of the main Hall. Among them the victors laughed drunkenly, swung their weapons, and jeered as they ordered the bodies of the dead carried away.

Bolton sized up the situation at once. He touched Nel's shoulder and whispered, "A mutiny. Tarl's men have taken the island. Not the first time...and not the last, I'll warrant, that it's happened here."

At that moment, Tarl emerged from the door of the Hall.

He carried something...a melon? No! The head of Captain Jacker, dangling long locks of red hair that were dabbled with blood, hung from Tarl's hand. The mouth was open, the tongue lolling out. The dead eyes gleamed in the torchlight.

There was a hushed murmur, sounds of shock and even anger. But the naked steel in the hands of Tarl's henchmen quelled any thought of protest.

Tarl stepped closer to the crowd. "You want to follow Jacker, just come on. Now," he challenged.

Bolton fumbled for the dirk at his belt. "I'll split the bastard, I will," he muttered, as he pushed against the line of backs ahead of him. "Cap'n Jack was me mate."

Nel thrust out his foot, caught the wooden leg as it moved forward, and sent Bolton sprawling. The old man cursed with rage, trying to rise, and the crowd laughed nervously, but Nel bent to help him up and whispered. "You can't whip 'em all. Be still!"

The drink still had the old man befuddled. "Jack was me mate!" he said,

"So what good is it going to do you if you follow him into the grave?"

A hint of understanding came into the watery eyes.

"What's going on back there?" It was Tarl, craning to see over the heads of those between. Luckily, the crowd had hidden the incident.

"Bolton One-leg! You back there?"

Nel nudged the old man. He managed to reply. "Aye. 'Tis Bolton." His tone was so chilly that even Tarl, hot with victory, should have recognized it.

Tarl growled. "What say you? You were Jacker's man. What say you now?"

Nel stared frantically at the old man. Bolton shook his head in resignation. "I follow no dead man."

Tarl knew that the crowd would follow Bolton. He leaned forward with the intensity of his desire. "You swear that?"

"I do."

"And the rest of you...who say you is the new cap'n?"

Nel shivered as a shout of "Cap'n Tarl!" went up from the throng. The light from the torches lit Tarl's eyes to flame, and he handed the bloody head to one of his men. "Put this on a post for all to see."

A silver flash moved in the torchlight, quenching itself in Tarl's shoulder. He roared, falling back into the arms of some of his men.

"Who?" someone roared.

Some were staring upward, along the flight-path of the knife. A lonely figure stood on the barracks roof.

"You bastards!" It was Dida, of course, alone and defiant as always.

"Get her!" one of the new captains grunted. "Now!"

The taunting voice drifted down. "I'll get you, Tarl! One night, while you sleep, I'll cut your filthy heart out!" Then she was gone.

Tarl wrenched the blade from his flesh, wiping the blade on his tunic. He held it up. "This blade finds her hide...or yours, take your pick. Bring me no excuses!"

His followers disappeared in a rush. Tarl was learning quickly that fear was a powerful motivator. He turned to the crowd. "Go home!" he shouted. The throng dispersed into their holes as if by magic.

Bolton was chuckling under his breath. "What's so funny?" asked Nel. He closed their door behind them and kindled a fire. It was near dawn, and he couldn't imagine ever being sleepy again.

"That Dida...just like her Pa. Has grits, she does."

"Seems to me she acted stupid."

"Don't your folk avenge their kin?" Bolton's tone was sharp, now. His faded eyes looked angry.

Nel struck the flint. A spark caught in the hay under the kindling. "Your people killed my parents." He didn't glance at Bolton. "You think I ought to take out after all of you on the island, kill until I'm killed? That would be dumb." Nel blew hard, and the flames grew and danced.

"When you first brought me here, that was all I could think about. Killing Hawkers. Burning their houses. Throwing their children into the sea. But I don't have to do that. You're going to do it to yourselves, without my ever lifting a hand. I can see that all I ever had to do was wait, and I'll have my revenge. Now I just want to go home. Tarl and his gang have done my work for me. And they'll get theirs, too, sooner or later."

Bolton stared at him as if he had never seen the boy before. For the first time there was a grudging gleam of amusement in the squinted eyes. "You kep' it mighty close, what you felt," he said. "I didn't know...."

"You want me to shout it from the housetops like that fool Dida? I'd have been fish bait long before now, if I had. That's a thing I learned from my folks...bide your time. Control yourself. Think before you act. It'll get you a lot more than swashbuckling around, making a lot of noise."

Bolton shook his head. "Not much chance of your getting home now. With Jack you might've earned your freedom. With Tarl...I'd guess nobody will be free as long as he's alive. We're all in for bad weather, I suspect."

Nel looked up. "Why did he kill Jack, Bolton? What reason could have made him do it?"

Bolton hobbled to his bunk and sat. He eased the stump above the peg leg and ran his hand through his stubbly hair. "That do be the question. And I think the answer may be mightily ugly, if we ever learn it."

* * * * * * *

Tarl grimaced as his lieutenant tightened the bandage about his shoulder. "Well enough, now. Leave it. I've had worse. Did anyone find that little bitch of a Dida?"

"No, sir."

His lieutenant trembled as Tarl snarled in anger. Then the new captain's face cleared and he said, "I have a job for you, Chukker. In the morning, be ready."

The man, relaxing, looked up. "Aye, Cap'n."

"Take two men over to our hidden anchorage near Portland. Find that man Slator. Tell him things have changed on Blood Island."

Chukker nodded. "Anything else?"

"Tell him it's time we met again. This time there's a cap'n here who's interested in that plan of his."

* * * * * * *

138

Nel could hardly believe that the Seahawks would accept the change in their leadership with such apathy. After that bloody dawn, they settled into their old routine as if nothing had occurred.

In Dover, such a thing would have caused continual upheaval, rebellion, and general unrest. Months or even years would have been required to settle the people again into their old lives. The Hawkers, in contrast, seemed used to violent changes. They were little concerned with the move from one leader to another, as long as the prospect of loot and action was there.

Only the search for Dida had not been resolved. Tongues wagged. Search parties went out by night and by day, and they all returned empty-handed. After a week, stories began circulating.

She had stolen a skiff and escaped to the mainland. That idea was quashed when a careful count was made and no skiff was missing. Then someone suggested that her father might have had a private boat hidden in some secret spot they hadn't located. That gave rise to another speculation: She might be hiding in a natural grotto. The island was large, mostly unexplored, and known to have many caverns cut into its cliffs by the pounding seas of the Atlantic. Some of the older Hawkers swore the northern side of the island was honeycombed with such caves.

The new captain ignored the gossip. His failure to capture a single teen-aged girl rankled, and he kept searchers busy. He offered a reward to anyone bringing a clue, but nothing came of that, either.

As time went by, Tarl grew agitated with the failure. He seemed to have the opinion shared by many others that the girl was quite capable of carrying out her threat. Most believed that he slept, nowadays, with one eye open.

The winds turned again from the south. The weather warmed, and outdoor activities were resumed. Nel fell into the familiar pace easily and went through his training sessions, marveling at how much stronger he was than he had been two years before.

He had grown...now he was not far short of his father's

inches. His frame was filling out, hinting that he might equal his father's strength in years to come. His muscles were hard, and he had the endurance many others still lacked. Bolton bragged that he was the best runner in the community, and Nel grinned and said nothing. Such abilities might help him escape, in time to come.

Strangely, he often found himself thinking about Dida. Their situations were now reversed. She was now in the same solitary position he had known when he first arrived. He wondered if she felt that desperation, that loneliness. If she were, indeed, still alive. Unless she had found some source of food and shelter, she could not have lived through winter's raging end.

It had never occurred to him that he might be the one to find her, so that event took him totally by surprise. He was nearing the end in his long run around the Island, just after sunrise. As he came round a bend of the hilly path he saw a dark shape move only yards ahead. An animal? He peered sharply. No. That shadow moved up the incline, its shape becoming clear against the brightening sky.

It was Dida!

Forgetting that he was already tired, he leaped up the slope after the scurrying figure. Dida scrambled over ledges and rocks like a spider, moving with the confidence of one in her own element. Nel was not as expert. He fell more than once, but he kept going, hoping to catch up to the fleeing girl.

As they moved up the cliffs, he could tell that she was beginning to flag. The gap between them shrank. With a burst of speed, he rounded a cluster of boulders into which she had disappeared. She wasn't there. He leaned against one and tried to catch his breath. Where could she have gone?

At that moment a bundle of sweaty flesh and stringy hair dropped onto him from above. Her fingers dug for his eyes. One knee jabbed at his groin, as they rolled.

"Dida! Quit!"

"Nel?" She put a knee onto his chest and sat up to stare at him. He raised a hand to brush some of the grit from eyes.

"It is you, Nel. Give me any trouble, and I'll smash you!" She lifted a sizeable rock and held it above his face.

140

Nel looked at the rock. Then he looked at Dida. She was so dirty he barely recognized her. Her eyes were gaunt and sunken, the long brown hair a mess of tangles and snarls. Her clothing was so badly torn it was a wonder it held together.

"You're a mess," he observed.

"None of your business!" she snapped.

"Will you get off?" he groaned.

She didn't move. "Why did you come after me? You want Tarl's bag of gold?"

Nel found himself getting irritated. "For someone as old as you, you surely do act like a baby."

"I can take care of myself."

As she spoke, Nel twisted violently to one side, pushing her hard with both hands. She rolled into the dirt, still holding the rock. He sat up and laughed.

"Don't brag. I didn't come up here to fight, anyway. If you'll relax a little, I want to talk to you."

Dida sat and studied him. Then she put down the rock. "We've got nothing to talk *about*."

Nel rose to his feet. "Then that's fine. I wanted to see if I could help you, somehow, but if that's the way you feel...."

"That's a laugh! Why should you help me? I've done nothing but make your life hell since you've been here."

"You did. But that sort of kept me going. Getting so mad at you let me forget how miserable I really was. I guess just lately I've seen that. Now, with what happened, I thought maybe I could do something for you."

Dida stood and faced him. He could see the hate in her eyes. It reminded him of his own, when he first came here. "I can handle myself and Tarl. Both," she said. "You just watch me!"

"So starving to death is going to get back at Tarl. I can just see him crying! Sooner or later, some of his men are going to find you, you know. I just did, and I wasn't even looking for you."

She flinched, but her glare was still full of fury. "I don't need you!"

"Well, you need somebody. Look, Dida, they killed my dad, too. I figure that puts us on the same side, like it or not, If you want. I'll go to Bolton. He'll help you. He's still your father's man, no matter what he has to say to Tarl."

"I can believe that," Dida said. "Pa always liked old One-leg. But us on the same side? That's hard to swallow, dirt-grubber."

"Call me Nel. That's my name."

Dida did the one thing he was completely unprepared for. Her face wrinkled up, and she began to cry. He moved toward her. She shrank from him at first, then leaned into his arms, her body racked with grief.

He didn't know what to do. So he hugged her gently until she could control her sobs. He could feel her wiping her tears against his shirt.

"You can ask Bolton, if you really want to," she muttered against his shoulder."

* * * * * * *

It was no problem to enlist the old man's help. As soon as he got back to the quarters they shared at the end of the day, he poured out his story.

Bolton was attentive. "Where's young Dida now?" he asked.

"Up in the cliffs. I told her that if you agreed, we'd come after dark."

Bolton scratched his stubble of beard. "Best you go alone. Two of us monkeying around're more likely to get caught. 'Sides, this wooden foot's not the quietest thing to sneak about on. You go quick, bring her back to shelter."

Nel gazed about the small room. He shook his head. "Here? There's hardly enough room for the two of us. If they search again, how will we hide her?"

The pirate grinned, his snaggled teeth glinting. He pointed to the table in the center of the small space. "Pull that toward your bunk. I'll show you something."

Nel did as ordered. Bolton jerked up from his bed to kneel on his good knee. Bending, he swept aside the dust and debris to clear the floor. Then he dug in his nails about a slab that seemed to be flush against the next.

He pulled. The planking opened to reveal a dark gap. Nel knelt beside Bolton to stare down.

142

"A hole!"

"Bright lad!" chortled Bolton. He peeled away another plank, and Nel found himself looking into a rock-lined passage.

"The caves, my boy. Dug out of the island's guts since the beginning of time by the tides. Jacker and I found out about 'em when we built quarters for Dan'l Tooth, years and years ago. Kept 'em secret from all but a few. I'm the last of those. Seems a fit place to hide Jack's whelp, don't it?"

* * * * * * *

Nobody saw Nel as he went, a flitting shadow speeding down the guttered paths and away to the hills. No roving sentry caught a glimpse of the two of them when, later, they returned over the western wall, flitting down the dim alleys to One-leg's quarters.

Once they were safely inside, the frightened, half-starved child found herself warmed and fed for the first time in what seemed forever. Here, for the time being, Dida found sanctuary.

CHAPTER FOURTEEN

Koola felt danger in the air. It was near and compelling. As he urged Gray his Wolfhound into a trot, he gazed from side to side, his head swiveling back and forth, his bright eyes busy. He had followed this rocky track away from the rest of the patrol. The wisdom of that was now in doubt, because they were hours behind him. He was farther north than anyone had come since Gem's disappearance, and he had kept going, drawn on by a hunch.

His intuitions, with those of his kind, were more reliable than any hunch of the human sort. His Macaque talents had brought him into these mountains. This meant something, even if the same senses told him that danger was all about. He kept his hand on his sword-hilt as Gray moved among the crags. There was a scuffling sound, and before he could hide a large furred shape barreled down the path toward him.

Recovering from his momentary scare, Koola gave a bounce in the saddle. "Merry! Good girl, Merry. Koola glad you found!"

He rode up beside the bearfox, controlling Gray's reluctance. "Move, dog! Merry friend. You see!"

Merry raised her head for Koola to scratch beneath her neck. "Now. Where Small-boots? You find, okay?"

The golden eyes looked into Koola's. He knew she understood him. "Yes! Yes, take Koola to Gem."

Merry growled softly and turned back on her own track. Koola kicked his dog into motion behind her. As they sped along, he was so happy at his discovery that he forgot his earlier qualms.

If he had been alert, he would have known that behind him someone had crossed his trail. Not one of First Dog

144

men...a hostile. That was what his instinct had tried to warn him about.

Gray was hard put to keep up with Merry. The way was steep and rocky, hard for her, burdened with a rider. Yet she gave her best, and Koola had a hard time keeping his seat as she leaped chasms and dodged outcrops of stone. Within a short while, Merry came to a stop at the entrance to a cave. A wisp of smoke curled from the opening. Koola dropped from his saddle and ran toward the cave.

"Small-boots?"

"Koola?" Gem stumbled from the rear of the cave, face dark with smoke and lined with weariness. On seeing her old friend, the tense expression eased. She dropped to her knees to hug the Macaque.

He stepped back to point at her shoulder. "You hurt? Is bad?"

"No. Almost healed now."

"Kray's people do this?"

"No, no. A rock-cat. We've been holed up here for almost a week, I think. I was out for a while, at first—blood-loss. But Berry took the worst of it. He's still bad off."

"You have supplies? Not able to hunt like that." Gem whistled to Merry. The bearfox nuzzled her arm as she rubbed her ears. "Merry hunted for us all. She brought in game—wild turkeys, hares. Once I was able to make a fire, we didn't have to eat it raw; that helped. But that's not important. We found the outlaw camp!"

"You find Kray?"

"Just before the rock-cat got us. You've got to get First Dog up here soon."

Suddenly the Macaque's eyes narrowed. He went rigid. "Small-boots!" he whispered. "Trouble come, very fast. Outlaws. V'ry close. Come this way, right now."

Gem freed her sword. "We can handle them."

"Too many. Small-boots take Merry and go."

"No!"

"Koola's dog tired. Too tired to run. You see?"

"Then we'll double on Merry. You're not that heavy."

"Make us slow. They catch. This only way. Go to Kenteen, bring troop to catch bad Macaque. Else all we do is lost. No good. Small-boots go?"

She knew he was right. The location of Kray's camp was the important thing, and she could bring the troop to it.

"I hate it when you're right all the time."

"I tell Cormal that, too."

She saddled Merry swiftly. Koola drew his blade and laughed. "Fight like wild dog. Bad men cry plenty."

She looked down at him, her eyes damp. She kissed the leathery cheek. "I'll be back with help. Soon, I promise."

"Now go fast. Koola feeling v'ry strong."

Gem knelt to hug Berry. The beast's eyes shone in the dimness, but she felt that he understood what was going on. "Take care of Koola, if you can," she murmured. Then she sprang into the saddle.

Gem heeled Merry in the direction Koola pointed. "Give 'em hell, Koola," she cried. Then she was gone, leaving Koola feeling proud as he faced the sounds of oncoming dogs.

They came headlong, without caution. When the first few were clear of the trees, he had no time to count them. They were yapping blurs all about him. He swung his sword again and again, feeling it bite into flesh and bone. The howls of pain rose from men and dogs alike.

"Watch him!" a voice called.

"Spit the monkey!"

Koola ducked a blade and sliced into the arm wielding it.

"Take him alive!" came a shout. "Alive, dammit!"

He shuddered at the thought of being captured by such men. He intended to die fighting. It would be well worth it if First Dog were given the time to get their crack at Kray's band. He fought more determinedly, his energy seeming endless.

Gray barked ferociously, dodging among his assailants. Her yelps brought unexpected results. Berry rolled out of the cave. He moved slowly, with effort, but with grim determination. He plowed into a cluster of riders, and the bunch scattered at the sight of him. One rider was a second too slow. A massive paw swept him from his saddle. Another swipe smashed him flat.

146

Finding he had an ally. Koola became amazingly cheerful. Yet he remembered what Gem had said about Berry's condition. Koola leaped from Gray's back and retreated to the bearfox's side. He knew, once he saw the terrible scars, and half-healed wounds, that the animal could stand only a short fight.

Before long, the outlaws saw it, too. Against a well and angry bearfox, they would have turned tail and run home. This one was wounded and weak. Three longbows let fly. Berry roared with agony, but he lumbered toward his assailants. Another barrage greeted him. Prickled with arrows, he collapsed into a heap. Koola, beside him, went berserk. Seeing Berry dying was more than he could bear.

He charged the bowmen, his blade busy. His first victim showered him with blood as he toppled from the saddle. Koola turned to another...and something hit him from behind. Even as he fell unconscious, the pain of Berry's death was greater than that of his own.

* * * * * * *

Gem pushed Merry harder and faster than ever before. They fled down the twisting path, as the shadows of noon lengthened into early evening.

Clinging to the heaving beast, Gem was glad that spring was on its way; the days were longer. When it became dark, she would have to slow her bearfox or risk injury to both of them. Even that concession went against her inclinations. Koola needed aid immediately. She did not intend to rest until she came to Kenteen's winter camp.

She burst from the mountainside into the level forest amid a skittering of startled birds. She was numb from the waist down, except for her knees, which ached abominably. Her arms were almost too heavy to handle the reins.

She could feel the laboring of Merry's lungs, but the bearfox was still putting everything she had into her efforts. She'd continue, Gem knew, until she dropped. If they were to reach their goal, they had to pause for rest.

"Whoa, girl. Easy now." Gem gentled her to a halt at the edge of a little meadow. She dismounted and took down the water bag. After a long swallow for herself, she cupped her hands, holding the pouch beneath one arm, braced against a raised knee. Despite the pain in her injured arm, she cupped her hands and offered water to the thirsty animal.

They rested. Gem surveyed the surrounding countryside, thinking it looked familiar. Yes, she recognized a warped tree at the forest's edge. There was a group of saplings with a dead one in the middle. She knew where she was.

The pine forest before them was growing darker now, but it was one she had traveled before. As night overtook them, she urged Merry into a trot again and set off down a path through the wood. The path forked ahead, she recalled. She must take the left branch. As she approached, she heard something...a yapping of dogs. The troop? Or Kray's men?

She glimpsed the colors of First Dog through the trees. A patrol of Kenteen's own troop, in fact. She stood in her stirrups and yelled. She didn't halt to explain matters but urged Merry onward. The soldiers sped after her, and Sergeant Lanse came up alongside Merry.

"I've got to find Kenteen as soon as possible," Gem told him. "Right now I'm too tired to talk." He nodded, and was silent as she endured the final moments of that wild ride with sheer willpower.

The patrol had, she knew, been searching for Koola. As they approached the fort, Gem lifted her head. One of Sergeant Lanse's men ventured to speak to her.

"The major is going to be happy to see you."

Gem smiled wearily. "He's going to be even happier when I tell him how to find Kray's headquarters."

The man looked stunned, and Sergeant Lanse grunted with approval.

"I had to leave Koola. If he's not dead, he soon will be... he was outnumbered. I just know it."

Sergeant Lanse caught his breath. "Quick-trot!" he roared, and his men brought their walking animals back to a trot. Gem's impatience infected the men and the animals as they covered the remaining ground and entered the barricade. She had to keep believing that she was in time.

* * * * * * *

Koola opened his eyes into harsh torchlight illuminating
a huge cavern. He squinted, then shut them again. His head
was spinning from the blow that had sent him into darkness.
The noise of many people echoing through the system of
caverns must, he thought, have waked him. Glancing through
slitted eyelids, he saw people passing an open arch. Many of
them...too many. Smoke tanged the dusty air. Smells of
cooking and leather and men and dogs. He shook his head,
only to find it jangling with the worst headache he could recall having in all his life.

He was hanging from his wrists, and his arms were
stretched between a pair of wooden stakes. His feet barely
touched the rough stone of the floor. He closed his eyes, remembering that final battle. So now he was a prisoner. He
didn't dwell upon what might await him.

He peered about cautiously. The cave was the headquarters Gem had seen. It had to be huge, from the numbers of
people marching within his sight. They would have him deep
in the complex, he was sure.

"Hey, Galik, he's awake!" said a voice. "Get the chief."

A pot-bellied man came into view from behind him, and
he ran out into the part of the passage Koola could see.
Koola wondered if he should have pretended to be unconscious a while longer...but that would just have postponed
the inevitable. Like it or not, he was in the worst pickle of his
less-than-respectable life. All the dubious ventures he had
entered into before had left him unscathed. Just this unselfish
act of bravery had put him into the soup. He had never felt
less heroic.

He was scared stiff, from the ruff of fur atop his head to
the toes of his odd-shaped boots. Even as he admitted this
fear to himself, it seemed to calm him. He knew that what
would happen would happen. To quake with terror was
pointless. His kind understood death, far better than did his
human friends, he thought. Pain...well, pain was a part of
living. When you quit hurting, you had better check up on
yourself—you might just be dead.

He waited. A knot of men came into view entirely too
soon. They were led by a short figure in a black cloak...a

Macaque. Kray, without a doubt.

That harsh name suited its owner. The leathery face was scarred and twisted with more than the physical injury. Koola realized that he was in the presence of one of the really evil ones of his kind. He sensed the Macaque lacked those links with the natural world that made most of his sort decent and kindly. It set him apart from his species.

Now Kray was eye-to-eye with him. A sneer warped the face even further. Koola kept himself from flinching at the cruelty in the black eyes.

"So...this be Tailman ride with Portlanders, eh? Why you do that? No Tailman ever a dog-rider before this!"

Koola assumed his coolest expression. "No Tailman ever big bad outlaw before, either. You do that. I do this."

Kray frowned. "Kray first Tailman ever to make Man afraid!" he said harshly. "Kray strong. Kray smart. Make big men follow him."

Koola stifled a yawn. "Kray got big mouth."

A gasp rose from the Macaque's human followers. No one had ever talked back to Kray before. They understood his temper. Kray slapped Koola soundly across the face. His head rang even more loudly, and he tried to lunge, forgetting how tightly he was tied. Even so, the ferocity of his expression made Kray step back.

That bothered the outlaw chief. "Where is dog troop?" he shouted.

Koola would have liked to say that First Dog was getting very near and would probably fall upon Kray's hideout within hours. He would have enjoyed shaking the creature up again. But he held his tongue. He was relieved to find that Kray's men had not spotted the troopers. It might mean that Gem had not gotten through, but it might also mean that Kenteen was being properly cautious.

If he said too much, Kray might well pull his people farther into the mountains. Then, who knew if anyone would ever spot them again? Koola knew he had to hold his tongue. But he searched his memory for a biting retort that would cut a Macaque with particular appropriateness.

He fixed Kray with his bright eyes. Very slowly, with much emphasis, he said, "Your mother swing by her tail!"

150

Kray swelled with rage.

"You will tell! Kray make words come very quick. You see, dog-rider. Soon you see." He turned, his cloak swirling wide behind him. "Put men on watch on other side stream, Post high in cliffs. Must know if First Dog come near. Send patrols, double count. Kray want answers now!"

He took a dirk from its scabbard and went around behind his prisoner. "Now, stupid one, we see how long you keep mouth shut."

Koola tried to twist his neck to see what the Macaque was up to...but his tail was suddenly pulled tightly as a foot held its end to the floor. Kray must be standing on the end of it.

"Nice long tail, scout."

Koola had never been particularly vain, but he had liked his tail. Among his people, the length and color of *that* appendage were matters of significance, and his own was fine in those respects. A tailless Macaque was ridiculed. A chill shook him. He cursed in Macaque, the gutturals sputtering through the chamber.

Kray answered his curses with some of his own. Then he said, "One finger-length of tail for each day you not talk. Think on that, Scout."

Koola closed his lips, lowered his head, closed his eyes. He was caught in a nightmare, and there wasn't a thing he could do about it.

Kray laughed. There was a brutal pain at the end of Koola's long and beautiful tail. It didn't end but grew worse and worse. Then something was tightened just above the scat of the pain...a tourniquet must have stopped the flow of blood.

Koola gritted his teeth. At last the pain overcame him, and he screamed shrilly.

* * * * * * *

Kenteen looked up to see a patrol coming through the gates. He had not gone to his quarters after supper, for he was worried. The loss of Gem, the fruitless searches, then the loss of Koola had made him nervous.

151

He noted the tired dogs as they walked into the light of the watch fires. Among them was a bearfox! Merry!

Gem was riding her, but there was no sign of Berry. Kenteen counted his men...they were all there, except Koola. He hurried forward.

Cormal passed him, running toward Gem. Kenteen smiled as the scout scooped her from the saddle and hugged her in a fashion that could not be called brotherly. Jace had been right again. He wondered how he had ever gotten along without these two women.

He returned his officer's salute and looked the group over. "Gem...it is good to see you again."

"Major, I've found the outlaw camp. It's been a while, but we got into trouble and had to hole up until we healed enough to travel. Koola found us yesterday."

"Where is Koola now?" Kenteen found himself more concerned than he would have thought possible.

"The outlaws got him. Raiders followed him to my hideout. He sensed their approach, which is how I had time to get away. His dog was too tired to run, and if we had doubled up on Merry they'd have caught us. I had to come to give you directions to their camp. He stayed behind...to slow them down." She dashed a hand across her eyes.

Cormal drew a deep breath. "Is he dead?" he asked in a terrible voice.

"I don't know, Cormal. I had to leave him and Berry. We must get back, quickly. Maybe it's not too late to save him."

"Sergeant Lanse!" Kenteen was already organizing his troops for pulling out. "Sound general muster. Get the line officers to my quarters. We ride out in two hours, ready or not."

* * * * * * *

The knock on the head, with the loss of blood and the stifling smoke of the watch fires in the cave, had made Koola groggy and sick. He drifted through the first day in a pained daze. When Kray came again, knife at the ready, he willed himself to silence, even as the blade sliced deeply and Kray dangled another piece of his tail in front of him.

The outlaws would never see him whimper again.

He prayed to his strange Macaque gods that Gem had made it back to the troop. He prayed that the troop would come soon. If it didn't, there was no hope. Every day would bring another mutilation, more pain, until he was completely tailless. He would be an object of ridicule among his own people.

The gruel he had been fed threatened to come back up his throat. He quelled his stomach by willpower and deep breathing.

Kray faced him again, holding the bit of bloody tail. Koola's stomach heaved. Vomit spattered to the floor. Kray dropped the grisly trophy into the puddle and walked away, his laughter echoing around the stone chamber.

CHAPTER FIFTEEN

Tral One-eye hated guard duty. Walking the same path, day after day! It was useless, he thought. In six years of following Kray, he had never seen a time when hostiles had come within a week's march of the hideaway. Cold and stiff, he stamped noisily down the path for the hundredth time. The sun was up, had been for hours. He hoped his relief would be on time. He hadn't eaten all night.

Something gritted on stone behind him. He turned, expecting to see his relief. He faced a man on dogback, in uniform and armed. The guard's single eye goggled, his slow brain trying to catch up with events. His hands fumbled at his blade, raised it to skewer the dog in the chest...but another pair of hands caught him from the rear, about the throat. Something glinted...he never felt the steel that severed his jugular.

Cormal wiped his knife on the dead man's trousers. He nodded to Sergeant Lanse. This was the fifth sentry they had snookered. Without a word, they melted into the trees along the ridge to make their way back to Kenteen.

* * * * * * *

First Dog was concealed all over the plateau from which Gem had first spied the camp. The wall of evergreens gave good cover as they readied for the attack. The sentries on the cliff could not see them, and those afoot were now dead.

Cormal made his way past busy groups toward Kenteen's position. Gem and the officers were already bending over the sketches the girl had made and those the scouts had devised after scouting the hideaway thoroughly.

Gem was controlled, but Cormal could see that she was filled with grief. They had found Berry's body beside the trail. It had been evident that the gallant beast had died fighting. It had even touched the tough soldiers.

"Can we bury him properly when we are through?" she asked Kenteen.

"If we're alive to do it," Kenteen had replied.

That memory gave Cormal a special incentive as he scouted the camp. He had been the one to locate all the guards, both those on the ground and on the cliffs. Kray's men, he found, had grown careless with security.

When Cormal was the last to report in, Kenteen said, "Good work. Tell the units to mount up."

But Cormal shook his head. "It can't be done that way. Not by the book. We know they have Koola in that hole someplace."

"That's one reason for the attack—to rescue Koola," said the major.

"We won't get there in time. Once we cross that line of trees, one of those cutthroats is going to kill him. You know it. I know it."

Kenteen rubbed his chin. "How else can it be done? Sooner or later, Kray is going to send reliefs for those guards. Then the fat will be truly in the fire. I can't risk men's lives."

"Let me get down there before the fighting starts."

"How?"

"Look at me...my clothes are just like theirs. Hide and homespun. They're going and coming, busy. Who's to know I'm not one of them? There's too many for everybody to know everybody. I can amble right in as if I was one of 'em."

"Too dangerous. And what could you do if you did make it to Koola? You couldn't get back before we attack."

"Don't need to. If I can get to him, I can keep them from killing him until First Dog establishes dominance."

The major frowned.

"Koola hasn't a chance, any other way."

Gem nodded. "I'll go, too."

The major shook his head. "I can't risk two of my best

155

scouts on this crazy mission. Is that clear?"

Gem nodded.

Kenteen turned to Cormal. He pushed his dagger into the ground at their feet near a lump of rock. The shadow of the blade was a finger's length from the rock.

"When the shadow reaches the rock, we attack. Not a minute later. You have that long, Cormal. Good luck."

Cormal gave a hesitant smile. "See you below. Bye, Gem."

She smiled back. "Be careful, you idiot!"

Cormal laughed and turned to run down the trail toward the stream.

* * * * * * *

He had looked more confident than he had felt. Now Cormal felt terribly naked as he peered through the bushes along the creek. Men and women in rough garb were moving around in the area before him. Some girls were washing clothes on the rocks at the edge of the water, only yards from his position. He felt the stubble on his chin. He hoped he looked grubby enough to fit in with Kray's men.

He stepped across the creek. A girl looked up and giggled a comment to her companion. He ignored them and walked on past. Several boys with fishing poles dashed up the path, nearly colliding with him. An old man tending the dogs in the pens looked after the boys and made a blunt remark about their ancestry as Cormal passed him.

He nodded bored agreement and went ahead. His feet seemed to weigh tons. His back felt exposed. Then he was through the cave mouth, inside the high-arched tunnel.

He might just pull this off, after all.

In the dim light he proceeded cautiously. His gait remained unhurried. He was, he knew, surrounded by heartless murderers, but he kept himself in check. He had to find Koola. Several men emerged from a tunnel to his left. A furred shape led the group, and Cormal knew at once it was the Macaque. He slowed.

Kray glanced into his face as he neared. Cormal coughed, putting up a hand to shield his face a bit. He kept walking. He wanted to run. Kray might know he wasn't one of his men. But he kept to his slow gait.

He tried to reassure himself—the glance had been brief, and the Macaque had looked as if he were thinking of something else. There had been nothing in his eyes hinting at alarm. There was no point in getting spooked at this point.

Cormal turned into the tunnel from which Kray and his men had come. He kept close to the wall, taking careful note of every landmark. It might not be easy to find his way out again. A rock chamber came into view, but it held only an old woman lying on a pile of skins. He moved on. A second large stone recess came into view. A man sat against the wall at one side.

In the center of the chamber, Koola was spread-eagled from two posts. His head drooped on his chest; his mangled tail was curled about his feet, the bloody stump tied off with a dirty rag.

He looked dead. Cormal's heart seemed to drop into his stomach. He drew his blade and stepped quietly into the recess.

* * * * * * *

Kray had almost reached the main campfire in the big chamber when he realized that something had been troubling him as he came through the tunnels. What?

As his lieutenants talked, he had been unconsciously worrying at something in his mind. Someone. That man they had passed? He couldn't find a memory that matched the face. The man had been a stranger, though such a thought seemed preposterous. In the cave? Alone?

A spy...or someone intending to rescue the prisoner! Kray turned to his men. "Spy! In cave! Maybe dog-rider. Go. Look to Macaque prisoner!"

Before one of them could move, a chorus of yells distracted them all.

"Attack! We're under attack!"

He pushed through milling people, crying children, people trying to go deeper into the cave. Reaching the great arch of the cave mouth, he paused.

Impossible! But dog-riders were everywhere. The paths were full of them, and the glint of steel sparked in his court-yard, back across the stream, and even onto the farther slope. There were hundreds of men at his door!

Kray was no coward. If this was to be his end, he would make the soldiers pay dearly for it. "Kill the dog-riders!" he cried.

The troop had met only light resistance after crossing the creek. The surprise had been total. When Kray made his stand, however, things changed drastically. The riders hit a line of men braced by his resistance.

Steel clanged and lisped and whispered. The melee closed about Kray and his men.

* * * * * * *

Even as Cormal stepped into the room, shouts erupted far behind him. The guard began to rise. He went down, skewered on Cormal's blade.

Koola opened his eyes and looked up. "Cormal! Is you? Not dream?"

The scout cut the rope holding Koola to the posts. "Of course it's me. Who else would be crazy enough to come after somebody who'd take on Kray's army single-handed?"

He eased the Macaque down. Koola fell to his knees. Cormal knelt beside him.

"You all right?"

The big eyes looked sadly into his. "Tail mostly gone, friend Cormal! You see?"

"I saw, friend Koola. But if we don't get a move on, the rest of you is going to disappear along with it."

The pandemonium outside increased. There were a few of Kray's men still in the corridors of the cavern. Men ran past the tunnel opening without a glance for them. Nobody was thinking about escaped prisoners just now.

"Think you can make it?" Cormal put his arm around his friend.

The Macaque stood on his feet. He swayed, but they held him up. "Still can fight. Get dead man's sword."

As Cormal returned with the weapon, two men came

158

from a side passage and saw them. They ran forward as Cormal flung the long blade to Koola, hoping he would be able to manage the over-lengthy weapon.

Then he was busy with the pair. Cormal had not been trained in the finer techniques of swordsmanship, but his long reach and his ability to bluff served him well, and he used those skills to back the nearer outlaw into his companion. As the man retreated, Cormal tweaked the blade from the brigand's hand to send it sailing into the stone wall. Another swing ripped the fellow's face open. He dropped back, as his companion came forward.

Cormal retreated a pace. He could hear others coming to join the fracas. Too many feet were now pounding toward them. He wondered how Koola fared, and he spared a second glance toward the Macaque. Koola was braced against a wall, the sword held like a spear before him. That was the only way he could manage the long weapon.

Cormal felt something stab his hand, and he almost dropped his own weapon. His opponent danced forward, thinking he was disabled, but the scout was used to working with injuries. He whooped with anger and lunged.

The outlaw hadn't expected such an unorthodox reaction. He tripped as he stepped back. Cormal thrust through his exposed neck, and the man went down in time to free Cormal to step between Koola and the four men who were now surrounding him.

This was an entirely different situation. A blade nicked his cheek. His arm was tiring, letting those steel tongues nip too near his skin. Then, suddenly, one of the hooded men, shorter than the others, turned upon his mates and stabbed one of them deeply. Another, seeing a strange action from the corner of his eye, turned away from Koola to see what was happening. The Macaque sprang forward and drove his weapon through him. The remaining villain retreated, but another, arriving up the tunnel, joined him.

One of them attacked their erstwhile ally. The other came past to face Cormal and Koola. That was an error, for the pair cut him down from two sides at once. The mysterious outlaw was finishing up his own prey.

Stepping back, he flung back his hood. Gem's face came

into view. "I thought you'd need help," she said simply.

"Kenteen will have your hide!" Cormal grinned.

She laughed. "If we live that long. Look out!"

Another group had appeared at the tunnel's mouth. The three scouts set their backs together in a triangle and stood ready to greet the newcomers.

Koola laughed aloud. It was just like old times!

* * * * * * *

First Dog, too, was finding it like old times. Their weapons sang shrill songs of death. Kenteen had trained them well, and they were elite troopers. Following their major, who led the attack, they surged forward, each giving everything he had.

Kray fought like a demon, leading his force into the milling fray. But though the outlaws were skilled at guerrilla warfare, they found themselves faced with another game... one whose rules they had never learned. They hadn't the discipline to sustain such direct battle for long. Indeed, if maddened leadership could have turned the battle, Kray would have managed to do it. He seemed to be everywhere at once.

The two sides heaved back and forth, testing their mettle against each other. Dog-riders fell, and outlaws fell more frequently. In the end, it was the iron discipline of the militiamen that weighed most heavily. Their dogs, always an integral part of their group, fought on even when their riders fell.

That unnerved the raiders, who treated their own animals so cruelly that they had to ward off frequent attacks from their own mounts. It was as well for them that they were not riding their dogs.

At last the outlaws fell back, by ones and twos, breaking for the cliffs and the safety of the mountains beyond. When the last of them surrendered, Kenteen called off his troops.

The captives were thrust into the winter dog-quarters. Kenteen saw them secured, and then he set about investigating the camp he had conquered. He had lost many men in a costly victory. He hated the thought.

He rubbed his tired eyes with a bloodied hand and wondered if he would ever have the chance to experience peace.

A disturbance made him look up. Sergeant Lanse was riding toward him. A trooper rode beside him, and between their mounts hung a shape in a long cloak.

"We caught this rascal sneaking out along a back trail," said Lanse. "Thought you might want a word with him. Cormal and I invited him to come along with us."

Kenteen stared down at the drooping Macaque. He wanted to weep at the thought of the carnage this creature had caused. Instead, he laughed.

Those of his men standing nearby looked around at sound of his laughter. That was the release they needed, and a tremendous roar echoed among the peaks.

* * * * * * *

The flush of victory didn't last long. Gem took charge of the wounded, and Kenteen and his officers began rounding up the slaves, counting their prisoners, and bringing together the dead. Gem recruited women, who at first seemed unaware that they had been freed, to help with her makeshift "hospital."

Kenteen was amazed at the order she brought to tending the injured. Among those was Cormal, who had a bad cut on his hand and a worse one in his thigh. His expression, however, was smug.

"What's so funny?" asked the major.

"One down and two to go," said Cormal enigmatically.

"What?"

"Nadak was in the middle of that mess, major. Nadak, who helped to kill my cousins, long years ago on our Long Hunt. Now I lack only the other two...." He sighed and winced.

Gem shooed away the visitor and went to supervise the dressing of the wounds of the next in line. She had a firm hand with the trained army medics, who seemed not to mind working under her supervision. Kenteen knew that the end of hostilities was a time for healing differences between people. One of the best ways he knew was to care for your enemy's wounded, along with your own. Gem was huge help in that regard.

161

The fallen were buried in a common grave and their dogs in another, no less carefully prepared. Some of the outlaws volunteered to help with their own dead, who made up the largest number of those killed in the battle.

A captain was making a roster of captives. He asked carefully as to their names and the places from which they had come. By the end of the first day, he had listed three hundred and twenty men, both well and wounded, sixty-eight women, and fifty children under the age of fifteen. There were two hundred riding dogs, a herd of milch cows, and a flock of chickens that were too nervous and numerous to try counting.

Among the captives strutted Kray. His tail curled upward, billowing out the back of his tattered cloak. His defeat had not cowed him at all, it seemed.

The troops' cooks had labored long to produce a nourishing meal, after the efforts of the day. The enemy women and children were sent to eat first, then the men of First Dog, and then the outlaws, brought in small groups.

The latter seemed suspicious at first. But when they saw that their women and children had already been fed, they dug in. Once all the others were fed, Gem took a bowl of stew to Kenteen. He was studying the huge group of people for whom he was now responsible.

"What are you going to do with them?" she asked.

He sighed and took a bite of the stew. When he had swallowed, he said, "That's a hard question. When they sent me out to clean up this mess, they didn't tell me what to do if I caught an entire town's worth of people.

"We were supposed to end the outlaw threat to the route and to establish new settlements in the woods. We'd already set up some trading centers before you joined us. Now we've ended the outlaw problem, but another just as big seems to have taken its place."

He ate some more stew. "Maybe the solution lies in those original orders, after all. We might turn this into another permanent trading outpost. What do you think of that?"

She looked about the compound. "Not bad. It's certainly secure. It's well placed, too, between the coastal villages to the south and the Canadas to the north. A good stopping-off place for traders and travelers."

"I think so, too. We'll explore the possibilities after the trials and executions."

She looked up, startled. "Executions?"

"Tomorrow. Of the leaders only. The rest will be given the chance to swear allegiance to Portland town." He scraped the bottom of the bowl. "I expect the rest of them, along with some of our own people, to start the outpost."

"What about the dead, Major?"

"One ritual fire. We'll kindle it after supper."

"I wish Berry had been buried with the mounts of Dog," she said quietly.

He smiled. "It has been taken care of. I sent Sergeant Lanse and a squad, as soon as they were through eating. They have it all done."

Gem stood and leaned to kiss his cheek. "Thank you. Major. You're a good man." She spun on her heel and went to check on her hospital. Kenteen looked after her, thinking of Jace, back at the main camp with the others. Suddenly he missed her very much.

The funeral was simple but powerfully moving. Kenteen, after a few quiet words, lit the kindling piled atop the mass grave. Then, turning toward the fire, he said, "Some of these men were our brothers. Others we fought here, but we respect them. They died well, though for evil purposes." He kindled the fire over the mass grave.

Flames roared up from twin pyres, licked by the gusty north wind sweeping down the ravine.

Gem stood with Merry among the troopers. She felt no shame at the tears on her face. The men were also weeping unashamedly. A small hand slipped into hers. She looked down to see Koola, his monkey face orange with firelight.

"Berry die to save Koola. Koola much sad."

"I know," she gulped. She reached to pull his small, almost tailless body against her. His long arms wrapped about her waist, as they stood together and watched the fire.

* * * * * * *

The next day was overcast. Kenteen called his ranking

163

officers together after breakfast. They huddled for a long time. Everyone else knew that something important was going on, but it was Sergeant Lanse who told Gem, as they fed Merry down by the creek.

"They're going to hang the outlaw leaders," he said.

"Yes, he told me. But I never thought, somehow, that he'd do it."

"What else can he do? If we were nearer, they could be taken to Portland for trial before King's Court. Out here there's only the major. He's the law in the wilderness."

At the cave mouth, Kenteen was interviewing prisoners. He sorted out the leaders, as well as he could. He found that the women were willing to tell him what he wanted to know, for the simple reason that they were being treated well for the first time since they had been with the outlaw band.

Before long, he had a group of men marched out to stand trial. He left Kray alone in the pen.

Thunder muttered among the mountain peaks as the major took his place. "This is a court-martial, convened in the name of the King and his Council, to find the guilt in the matter of outlawry and rebellion against the King's peace and his subjects."

He looked down at the prisoners. "To some extent, every one of you is guilty. But the King is merciful and does not desire retribution against those who simply took orders. You who stand before me were co-conspirators with prisoner Kray, and are as guilty as he. I find you, by these proceedings, guilty as charged. I sentence you to death by hanging, to be carried out immediately."

Some of those just sentenced scuffled with the troopers near them, trying to break their bonds. One had to be knocked unconscious before they could quell him.

"March these men to the oaks," Kenteen said. "Hang them there, along the ridge."

In minutes, six twitching corpses dangled from the oak trees. The lesson was not lost upon those who watched, as Kenteen had intended. "Justice has been done," he said. "You others know how fitting this was. Now I am empowered to grant to you the King's amnesty. Any of you who swear loyalty to the royal monarch in Portland, total obedience to his laws, submission of your lives to his requirements may take advantage of this amnesty."

A toothless fellow pushed forward. "What happens if we don't?" he asked.

Kenteen gestured toward the ridge. "You join them."

Now he had their total attention. "All who wish to swear fidelity to the King, raise your hands."

Every hand went up unhesitatingly.

"Good. Before you're released to go about your new duties as subjects of the King, there is a last execution to be carried out." He nodded toward the pens.

A pair of troopers brought a struggling Kray to stand before him.

"Kray of the Macaque, do you have anything to say before I pass sentence upon you?"

The Macaque was chittering with rage. His small eyes squinted malevolently. He growled a string of curses.

Kenteen ignored his words. "I order you to hang for...."

"No!" Koola screamed, running toward Kenteen. His expression was frantic. "Not hang Kray. Too easy!"

"Koola, this villain must hang for his crimes. He can't be allowed to threaten the peace again."

"Yes, yes, but not so easy. Koola kill evil Tailman. Not hang! Koola owed this, you see?"

Kenteen showed no emotion. "I see your point. But this is a military tribunal, not a personal vendetta."

The Macaque shook his head. "Koola got little tail, now. Kray cut most off. See?" He turned to let the healing remnant show.

Cormal moved forward, making a passage for Gem, who followed. "Why not, Major? Justice will be served either way. They are of the same race. Koola feels shamed by Kray. Why not let them fight?"

Kenteen frowned.

Cormal went on. "It's a matter of honor. Kray mutilated Koola. Crippled him, to their way of thinking. If anyone deserves justice, it's Koola. And if Koola loses, you can hang Kray anyway."

Kenteen turned to Kray. "Are you willing to risk death?"

Kray spat into the dust. "No risk. Plenty fun! I kill stupid no-tail!" He laughed harshly.

"Sergeant Calver, arm them with shortswords."

"Be careful," Gem said quietly to the monkey-man.

Cormal patted the furry shoulder. "Hurry it up, will you? I'm tired of standing on this bum leg."

Koola grinned. A space was cleared for the combat and on the word Kray sprang at Koola. Koola leaped sideways, bringing up his blade in time to parry that of the other. They crouched, circling. Kray feinted to the right, twisted to his left when Koola began a response. The downswing missed Koola by a hair. The carry-through left Kray exposed. Koola spun, moving with eerie speed, driving his blade into Kray's stomach.

The two of them froze in place for an instant. Kray's eyes held profound shock and surprise, as the wounded Macaque glanced down to see the blood staining his clothing. Then Koola tugged his stained blade free. His opponent gurgled, clutching at his belly. He fell to his knees, bent down, and rolled forward. He lay, twitching, on the ground.

Lightning ripped through the sky. A flood of rain washed out the pooling blood. Koola dropped the borrowed shortsword into the mud beside Kray and turned blindly toward his friends.

* * * * * * *

The long-time outlaw encampment began to take on the feel and bustle of a normal frontier post. The outlaws and their families found to their amazement that life under the command of Kenteen was much more secure—even easier— than it had been under the iron hand of Kray.

Hunting schedules were set up. As spring softened the ground, land was broken for planting. A committee set up a temporary government. Word spread through the wilderness communities with amazing speed. One morning a group of nomad hunters appeared, ready to do business with this new trading post.

They assured Major Kenteen that a trading family was not many days behind him. This told the major that things were well in hand. He went back to his winter fort to get those he had left there, as well as to find the time to write out his very long report to General Tion. Even the official language he had to use couldn't conceal the excitement and danger of the months spent tracking and quelling Kray's band.

It was only as he came to the end, with its roll-call of those killed in action that he felt heavy-hearted. He wrote a letter to each family, however, and he asked General Tion to see that the names of the dead were inscribed on the Roll of Valor plaque in the barracks of First Dog in Portland.

He wrote:

> Unless specifically ordered back to Portland, I will remain in the wilderness with this new township. The integrity and security of our new outposts need to be established firmly. There are other outlaws in the forest, though Kray's group was the largest and best organized.
>
> My work is far from done. In fact, I would appreciate your consideration of my application for permanent assignment to Fort Koola, as we call this new town. I find that I am weary—getting old, perhaps—and would appreciate the chance of focusing my whole attention upon something so stimulating and constructive.
>
> Please give my warmest regards to the Royal Family. I hope that you and your wife are well.
>
> Dutifully yours,
>
> Kenteen

He paused to look past the flame of his candle at Jace, asleep in their bed. He wondered what she would say when the chaplain he had asked to be sent arrived. He suspected that she would be more than happy to marry him. There were others as well. Several of the rescued women had formed

167

attachments with some of his men that promised to be permanent.

He wrote a separate note introducing his special messengers. One of these was a Macaque named Koola. Another was a very special woman called Gem of Dover.

* * * * * * *

The day of departure for Portland came all too suddenly for Gem, although she was anxious to get on with her search for Nel. She checked her hospital over again and again. She bade farewell to the many troopers who had become her fast friends. Then it was time to pack her meager gear into Merry's saddlebags and join the patrol waiting in the middle of the compound. The time had come....

Much had happened since she had left Dover almost two years before. Randor had told her that she would change, and she knew now that he was correct.

As she tied the last strap, she took the bearfox's reins and led Merry out into the spring sunshine. It was a clear day. The air was fresh, scented with blooming plants. Cormal, using his cane, which was necessary because the wound to his leg had not yet healed, stepped from the crowd. "I wish you could stay until I'm able to travel!" he said gruffly.

She looked up into his frank face and sighed. "So do I. But it's time and past time. The patrol can't wait, and I have to take this chance to get to Portland. I've waited too long, already. Nel will be almost thirteen—imagine it!"

He nodded. Glancing at Merry's gear, he said, "Looks like you're all set. Need anything at all?"

"Nothing that I can have right now."

He understood at once. "I'll come, just as soon as this leg is strong enough. I promise."

She shook her head, her long tail of hair swinging. "No. Don't come."

Hurt was written on his face.

"I want to come back here," she added. "After I find Nel."

He looked pleased, now. "You like it out here?"

"I do. These months have been the most exciting in my

life. They have given me purpose beyond that of finding Nel. I have outgrown Dover, I think. I suspect that Nel, if he is alive, has, too."

He grabbed her in a hug. "I'll be here. Waiting. I just wish I could come and help you."

She grinned at him. "So do I. But we'll come. Don't worry about that. Now I'd better go...I might do something stupid, like crying."

As she rode up to the waiting detachment, she knew that an unspoken promise had bonded them. Koola, waiting on Gray, had missed nothing. He grinned at her, his boot-button eyes twinkling.

"Now we go to Portland!" he said.

The captain saluted Kenteen. The column started out, and as they went through the gate and over the creek. Gem and Koola turned in their saddles to wave at Cormal, Jace, and Kenteen.

Then the wall intervened—and the trees—and they moved away toward Portland, amid the burgeoning spring.

CHAPTER SIXTEEN

Slator sat in the pirates' Hall, talking with the new lord of Blood Island. He was filled with glee, which he managed to conceal with some difficulty. Jacker was gone, that was the important thing, and these new men, Tarl especially, seemed to be cut from his own bolt of cloth.

Slator knew they would not worry themselves over the welfare of their own people, any more than over those in Portland. The chance of loot blinded them to danger. He turned up his mug and took another swallow of bitter ale. "You guarantee there'll be no monkeys left alive in the towers," Tarl said. "They'll all be dead by midnight, at the latest?"

"They will, I assure you. I'm now in charge of supplies. That includes food and water to the towers. Once I add my dose of medicine, the towers will pose no threat."

"The festival will be in full swing by the time we get there?"

"Correct. The Vernal Equinox is a festival of lights, celebrating the beginning of warm weather. The entire town will be out carousing all night. Half the garrison will be off duty. There will be fools parading around carrying candles, lighting up the town like noon."

Tarl smiled. "That's the part I like best. They'll be blazing away for my ships to home in on. Like sharks to dead meat!"

"Do you have enough time to get ready?" Slator asked,

Tarl stuck a filthy finger into his mouth and dislodged a chunk of meat, which he spat onto the floor. He laughed. "A week is enough. Even for the biggest raid ever. Right, lads?"

Chukker, sitting beside him, banged his empty mug on

the table. "Just give the order, Cap'n. The Hawks are with you."

There was a chorus of "ayes." Those sitting at the table yelled it vigorously.

"And that's when mighty Portland falls," Tarl growled.

Slator joined in the laughter. Soon, very soon, all his wrongs would be avenged.

Neither he nor his companions paid any attention to kitchen boys as they went and came. Nobody realized that one blond boy served at Tarl's table all evening.

Nel made his way back to Bolton's quarters very late. His heart was pounding with excitement. From the words he had overheard, he knew it was time for Dida and him to make their escape. When he reached the hut, he huddled over the fire with his sleepy companions, telling them the details of what he had learned.

Bolton didn't seem surprised. "I told ye. That's the reason Tarl took over the island. Old Jacker had too much savvy to fall for such a hare-brained scheme. But not Tarl. He's just as crazy as your Pa always thought he was, eh, Dida?"

Instead of going off like a train of gunpowder at the mention of Tarl, she nodded. She had changed a lot from the skinny waif Nel had rescued weeks before. With enough to eat, shelter from the weather, and time to rest, she had gained weight. Her vitality was once again at full pitch. For some strange reason, Nel thought she looked a lot different from the way she had all the time he had known her. Clean and fed and without a snarl on her face, she came near to being a nice-looking girl. Sometimes that thought almost made him nervous, but he had no time to reflect on such matters. He had more important things to discuss.

"That plan is crazy enough to work, Bolton. I listened close. If Slator poisons the monkeys, it could just come off."

"So?" the old man asked.

"Well, this place is going to be a madhouse for the next few days, right?"

"True. It will take all hands working hard to fit the ships for battle. Sails have to be mended. Weapons have to be put into order. Guess there won't be time to scrape the bows, though."

171

"With all this going on, who's going to miss one little skiff?"

Bolton looked at him with respect. "You're right, boy. It's the perfect time for you to get away. Can you handle a skiff?"

"If he can't, I can," said Dida. "I've handled boats since I was a babe. There's nothing I can't sail where I want to go."

Nel sighed. "That's just what I'd hoped you'd say. With you at the helm, we'll surely make it."

Dida looked momentarily as if she were going to say something sarcastic, but then she just smiled slightly.

Bolton poked the fire. "Then it's decided. All I have to do is get you a boat."

Nel looked up. "There's one more thing."

"What might that be?"

"You come with us."

Dida leaned forward, her face bright with firelight. "Yes, Bolton, you have to. No matter if Tarl takes Portland, he's never going to stop making life a living hell for all Pa's old chiefs. He hated you, Bolton, for years before he killed my father. Almost as much as he hates me."

"That's no secret," the old man said. "But I can't go, nevertheless."

"Why?" Nel asked.

"'Cause I'm a Hawker, boy. There be no other life for Bolton One-leg but the deck of a ship. To leave the sea...rot away on the mainland on some patch of dirt to grub, would be the death of me."

"But you'll probably die if you stay here, most likely at Tarl's hands."

"Aye, but it'll be a Hawker's death. Can't ask for more, d'ye see?"

The boy nodded. "It's your decision. I wish you luck."

"Luck to us all. Never thought I'd say that, but now we've got the same enemies, so I suspect we're friends. Time for shut-eye, anyway, if you're to get away."

* * * * * * *

172

When daylight came, Nel and Bolton moved around freely, performing their duties, and Bolton found a skiff with little trouble.

"A one-master," he said. "There's five anchored by the northwest docks."

"The fishing boats the old men use?" ask Dida.

"Aye. Everyone's working on the ships. None will look over at the fishing docks for the next few days. Tomorrow I'll go over them and pick the best for you."

"Then we might go tomorrow night?" Nel couldn't keep the excitement out of his voice.

"Right. No sense waiting. Where will you head for?"

The boy looked startled.

"Best steer clear of Portland," the old man said. "Make landfall south of the town, if you can."

"He's right," Dida agreed. "We don't want to be anywhere near Portland when Tarl sails in."

"Maybe we might head south toward Dover?"

"Dover...it's a long way. But if we stick to the shoreline we might make it," said Dida.

"Then that's the thing to do, my hearties. Now sleep. Ye'll need it tomorrow."

CHAPTER SEVENTEEN

Gem was sore from the saddle. The troop had been more than a month on the trail, and now they were nearing Portland. She found herself growing excited at the thought. She had never seen a town larger than Dover. And now Captain Dramus and the dog patrol had almost reached their destination.

Koola rode ahead of her, sitting peculiarly on the special padded saddle Cormal had made for him. The amputated tail had given the Macaque a bad time, and riding was painful. Even as she watched, he turned to look back and wave her up beside him.

"There. Portland be beyond." He moved with her to the top of Piermont Hill, and below them lay Portland with the sea beyond it.

Gem gazed down on the busy town. Never before had she seen so many buildings of so many sizes and shapes. They stretched along for miles.

"You could lose ten Dovers down there," she said to the Macaque. A salty breeze touched her face. Merry sniffed and shook her hide, rippling the reddish fur.

Full spring had seemed to follow them. The hills and forest were green, touched with colors of wildflowers. Birds twittered about them, and a few noisy gulls flew over their heads, aiming toward the waves beyond the city. The gulls reminded Gem of Dover. Home. Watching them swoop and glide, she felt suddenly that there might be a chance things would turn out well for her. Perhaps. She sighed.

"Portland, she beautiful, eh Small-boots?" asked Koola.

She nodded, still gazing down.

"I show Small-boots town. Is good place. Home Koola's

174

family." He touched Gray with his heel, as Dramus signaled for the patrol to move forward.

Around Gem, troopers were checking the alignment of their tunic buttons, smoothing their tousled hair, looking to their equipment. First Dog prided itself on looking sharp. They had camped, the night before, beside a river to wash and groom themselves and the dogs. Those with beards had washed them. Gem had washed her own long hair. Now it shone auburn in the sunlight.

A rider had been sent ahead to report to Tion. He should have arrived at least two days before the rest of the troop. Proving that he had arrived safely, the town was decked with banners and flowers. People, more people than she had ever dreamed existed, waited along the main boulevard and near the gates. As the dogriders passed through the gate, Gem found herself part of an occasion she would never forget.

She had expected more people than she was used to seeing, but the crowds filling the streets overwhelmed her. Macaques took perches on roofs and balconies by the hundreds, yelling greetings to their fellow, the Macaque who had killed the renegade Kray, cast out by his own people.

Koola chittered with laughter. Bands along the way played different tunes, which overlapped in increasing discord. Almost deafened, Gem realized that First Dog was dear to the hearts of the Portlanders, and the old town spared no effort to show its welcome.

Engrossed in watching girls throwing kisses and flowers to the troopers, Macaques cheering Koola, soldiers embracing their kin, Gem forgot that she might also be of interest to the jubilant throng. But so it proved.

Merry, in particular, roused much comment as they moved along. People kept wary eyes on the bearfox and gave her a wide berth as she passed by. Then a small boy, a mere toddler, dashed out of the crowd and sat down beneath Merry's nose. He flung wide his arms, as Merry gazed down at the small creature under her feet. She bent her neck to sniff at him, and the frantic mother, trapped in the crowd, shrieked despairingly. Merry looked the child over calmly. She let him wrap his hands in her fur to pull himself up to pet her. Then she sighed gustily and licked him on the nose.

The mother, sobbing hysterically, freed herself from the crowd and dashed to the street. But she stopped abruptly and stared at the animal. Creeping gingerly forward, she lifted the toddler in her arms. Timidly, she patted Merry and backed away into the crowd.

A cheer rose as Gem prodded the beast forward. "Show-off," she chided. "What am I going to do with you?"

A group of dignitaries waited for them in the military compound. The gates were opened as wide as they would go, and the throng followed the troop inside. There Captain Dramus dismounted, drawing his sword to present it to General Tion.

The general saluted the troop with the blade and returned it to Dramus. "Captain Dramus, acting for Major Kenteen, begs to report our mission completed as ordered, sir!" the captain barked.

"For Their Majesties, as well as the people of Portland, I welcome home this troop of First Dog. Well done." The general smiled.

"Dismiss your men. There will be celebrations and reunions with their families. You and your officers may come with me to my office."

"With your permission, I will bring Scouts Koola and Gem," said Dramus.

Gem followed the general into the office building. Dramus gave a brief report. Gem realized that the general was watching her and the Macaque with great interest.

They were taken on a tour of the compound, and found civic leaders waiting to meet the returnees. Portland relished the excitement of any dramatic event, and this was particularly welcome one.

As they moved past the throng, Koola twitched Gem's sleeve. "There," he said, pointing to an officer standing beside the barracks. "That Slator. We tell you about him."

Gem's gaze met that of the officer, and she felt a chill along her back. A weasely one, yet vicious, she thought at once. Cruel, narrow eyes...She shivered, and she felt Koola's hand, still on her sleeve, quiver in sympathy.

* * * * * * *

Slator watched the party disappear around the building. He was pondering this new twist in events. Reinforcements, only days before his proposed attack...but only twenty men. Surely that small number could make no real difference. He was glad to see the Macaque—that creature would have his personal attention, in time. And the girl...she looked like a tasty morsel. One he might save for himself.

* * * * * * *

After reading Kenteen's written report and listening to Dramus's in-depth account of the campaign, General Tion seemed even more impressed with Gem and Koola and their role in the suppression of the bandits.

He called them into his office, several days after their arrival, and explained to them the great value of the new settlements, as well as the land now open for colonization. "Portland owes you a debt," he told them. "If we can do anything to repay you, you have only to ask."

"There is one thing of great importance to me," Gem began. "My son...."

Tion nodded. "Kenteen explained your situation to me in his report. All our resources will be put to use in learning what we can. The King and Queen don't really like their unwilling alliance with the Hawkers. The slave trade is something we have hated, but allowing that traffic here is the only thing that has kept us from being frequent targets of the pirate attacks. Our informal treaty has kept the Hawkers from our waters."

"Yes. You are safe, while they prey on small places like Dover!"

He grunted. "You don't mince words!"

"General," she said. "I am not here to judge your royal family or you or the people of Portland. I want to find Nel. That is all I want, and for that I need help."

The general nodded. "You shall have it. When the Hawkers come in on their next scheduled slave and supply run, I shall inquire. If they still have him, we should be able to negotiate his return. If he is still...." His voice dwindled to

177

silence.

She understood him. If Nel was still alive. "I hope you can learn something, General."

Koola was tugging at her sleeve. "We eat now? Koola's stomach say it time for food!"

Tion smiled. "You will be my guests for dinner tonight. If you'd like to wash and rest beforehand, Corporal Mackern will bring you anything you like."

Afterwards, back in the twin rooms assigned to them in the civilian wing of the barracks, Gem washed and stood beside the window, thinking about her son. It had been so long...*was* he still alive? Where? She sighed as Koola came into the room.

"We big h'roes," The Macaque grinned broadly. "You know that? Never was before. It good feeling."

"Have you visited your family?" Gem asked him.

The little scout peeled off his cloak and dropped it onto the bed. "Got many kin, but all far off, like cousins. See them, but not much to talk about."

"You have no close kin at all?" Gem asked him.

The Macaque sighed. "Only Cormal and First Dog. Now they Koola's family."

He came to stand beside Gem, and they stared out over the palace garden, the great house of the royal family, the bay beyond. Somewhere out there, Gem thought. Nel, her own true family, was on an island—she hoped—out across the ocean beyond the headland.

* * * * * * *

The night was warm. Though the moon was invisible behind puffy gray clouds on the horizon, it colored the rest of the sky. Stars filled the dome of night. Beneath that bright canopy, Nel and Dida made their way with Bolton down to the fishing dock. They slid from shadow to shadow, as silent as the evening breeze. Just one man guarded the dock, and he was asleep. They stepped over him silently and sped onto the creaky planking.

Bolton's peg tended to thud loudly on wood. He did his best, hurrying them to the end of an arm of the dock, where small boats were tied up. "Hurry!" he warned. "They may be on us any instant."

He proved to be a good prophet. There came the sound of drunken laughter from the sheds on shore. Dida stared up, her eyes wide.

"Go!" Bolton's lips shaped the word.

Dida joined Nel in the craft.

A voice pierced the quiet of the night. "Hey! Who's out there?"

Bolton loosed the rope and threw it onto the stern. "Get moving!" he said.

Loud voices were coming nearer. Nel saw three shapes in the distance. "Bolton, come with us!"

"And miss a good fight?" He pushed the craft away from the dock. Dida dipped in the oars and pulled, as the old man turned toward those who were now crawling all too near.

"Someone's stealing a boat!"

"Stop! Hey, you in the boat! Stop!"

Bolton drew his cutlass. "Hold where you stand, mates. Or feel my steel."

"Hey, that's One-leg!"

Another voice yelled. "Hey! Jacker's pup's in the skiff!"

"Call Tarl!"

Before they could do anything at all, Bolton was upon them. The clang of metal pursued the skiff onto the dark water of the harbor.

Dida was straining every muscle to put distance between the skiff and the dock. As Nel continued to stare aft, the battling shapes dissolved into the darkness.

"Dammit, Nel, set the sail!"

"They'll kill him."

"He's a Hawker. It's the way he chose."

"Will they come after us?"

She was breathing deeply, timing her strokes. "Of course. Unless you get that sail up, they'll catch us, too."

Nel pulled down the pulley line, after releasing the crossbar. With a flutter and a snap, the canvas blossomed up and out, instantly filling with the brisk evening breeze. The craft shot forward. He crouched to fasten the line; then he helped Dida to take in the oars.

"You make a pretty good sailor," she said with none of her former begrudging tone.

He sat, his legs outstretched. "I've always loved the sea. I would have enjoyed the life on the island, if it hadn't been for your people killing my own family."

"No stomach for killing?" Her tone was scornful.

"Not really. Have you?"

"Pa said that it's the strong who live, in this world. The weak haven't a chance. I guess that means killing, too."

"It doesn't mean you have to like it."

She stared at him through the starlight. There was an odd expression on her face. "I guess not.... You always say such dumb thi...."

"Sssh! Listen!"

They strained their ears. The clang of steel on steel stopped. They could hear nothing but the pounding of surf on stone and the cries of occasional gulls.

Nel's breath caught in his throat. "It's finished. He... he's...." But he couldn't speak. Once again he had lost the nearest thing to a family he had. It seemed to be the pattern of his life.

* * * * * * *

The wind took them quickly out of the harbor, across moon-tipped waves. Dida, her hand on the tiller, watched behind them. Her sharp eyes caught a darker dot against the foam-flecked water moving toward them.

"A big sail," she said.

"Well...maybe the jump we got on them will be enough to let us make some kind of landfall."

The race was on. Lost in their own thoughts, the two were silent as they worked the skiff over the calm seas. The sail behind them grew larger, as it cut down the distance between the two craft.

By midnight, the clouds thinned to nothing. A fat white moon hung over them. Nel replaced Dida at the tiller and kept them, under her direction, on the right heading. They were tired, discouraged at the continuing pressure of the sail behind them. But neither would admit it, and they went on, for there was no alternative.

The pirates' boat had drawn so near they could see shapes of men gathered in the bow. "It won't be long now," said Nel.

Dida signaled for silence.

Nel listened. At first he could hear only the same sounds of the waves and breeze that had been with them all night. Then there was another sort of noise. A soft grating and swashing.

"Surf?" he asked.

"Can't be. We're nowhere near land."

"Then what?" Even as he spoke, the bow smacked solidly into something and burst. They were in the water, amid the remains of the skiff. As he went under, Nel heard Dida yell, "Reef!"

The chilly water stung Nel's tiredness away and moved him to action. He kicked hard and swam to the surface. Blinking his eyes clear of water, he saw bits of the boat all around him. Just ahead, the sinuous line of the reef glittered in the moonlight...it was a long rock that winked into view between waves. Dida sputtered to the surface, a few yards away. He swam over to her.

"Looks like we're in for it," he gasped.

As they bobbed up and down, they could see that the other ship had put about when the reef had come into view. Now it was anchored to seaward with men on deck trying to peer into the dark waters.

"Catch a board," Dida hissed. "Don't move too fast, just float naturally. Maybe they won't spot us."

Nel caught a jagged bit of plank and paddled beside Dida. Together they floated, letting the tide carry them past the reef, into open water again. Now they heard plainly the voices of men shouting. "Chukker, they be drowned!"

"Seems so. But what if they're not?"

"You saw that skiff. It ripped clean apart. Even if they be afloat, it's too far from land for 'em to swim. They'd never make it."

"True. We've wasted too much time already. They're dead, or as good as. Come about. Head for home."

The boat heeled away into the wind, tacking toward the

island. The two were elated, but it didn't last long.

"How far to land?" asked Nel.

"In the skiff we could have made it by midday. Now I don't know if we can make it at all."

Nel grunted. "Don't say that. We'll make it. Both of us. I'm the best swimmer in all these parts."

Dida snorted. "Who said?"

"Bolton, that's who. Nobody ever beat me in all the time I was in training."

"You never raced *me!*"

"You're a girl...that'd be no contest at all."

Her face flashed pale between swells. "Dirt-grubber! We'll see who makes shore first. Want to bet on it?"

"Sure," he said, pushing his plank ahead and kicking to propel it forward.

Dida kicked, too. They started off together.

After what seemed days, but had to be hours, the sky paled to mauve. Then it turned yellow with agonizing slowness.

A new day began.

182

CHAPTER EIGHTEEN

Any Macaque who loved water—particularly the undrinkable and undependable ocean sort—was considered very odd by his fellows. The Macaque had originated in the treetops of jungles far to the south. Most found the safety of congested towns or the green havens of forests the only comfortable places to live. As for wide expanses of empty water under no less empty skies—that was terribly unnatural to Macaque. So it was to be expected that when Mik chose to become a fisherman at an early age, he was immediately christened Mad Mik by the others in his family.

He didn't let their scoffing deter him. He served apprenticeship with several fine old sailors and fishermen who were considered masters of their skills. Now he himself was considered to be very good at his calling. He had hoarded his earnings to buy his own boat, and he went into business for himself. The hard, lonely life suited him, and in time even his friends and family learned to accept this eccentricity.

Mik was not a deep water fisherman. He cast his nets and set his traps close to the shoreline, for he liked working alone. Anyone going into the deep by himself was not only mad, he was suicidal. So it was that he took his accustomed route northward along the coast on a gloriously sunny day. As he worked the nets, he sang loudly. The gulls shrieked above him in accompaniment. He had taken a good catch. Soon it would be time to turn and head for home. As he pulled in the last netful, he caught sight of something bobbing in the distance. He squinted, trying to see it clearly.

"By the Great Long Tail!" he said at last. "It's someone swimming! Why anyone do that?"

There were two, he saw soon enough, both clinging to

planks. The pair looked exhausted, and he knew they were in trouble. He hauled in the last of his nets and caught up the oars, then strained to reach the weary swimmers. He paused when he was almost on top of them and looked down into the weariest young human faces he had ever seen. He reached for the first, but the boy gestured toward the girl.

"Get Dida!" he gasped. "She's...done in."

Mik reached his long monkey arms to catch the girl's plank, pulling her alongside. She had just strength enough to hold on. He took her under the arms and dragged her into the boat. The boy pushed her from below. Dida spilled onto the pile of fish.

Mik caught the boy's hand. This one was heavier, and the Macaque said. "Pull, boy, or you'll be fish food f'r sure."

Nel thought he had no strength left. But the thought of failing now, when they had made it, gave him new energy. He heaved himself up out of the sucking water. Mik hauled, too, landing him next to Dida. The stink of fish seemed heavenly.

Mik stared at his strange catch. "You be lucky not drown. What you do, go too far out?"

Nel had now regained a bit of wind. "Escaped...from Blood Island." He struggled to sit. Dida was doing same.

Mik jumped. "You get away fr'm pirates?"

"They thought we drowned when our boat went down. They went back to the island."

Mik stopped looking about for a raiding vessel. "That good. Me Mik. Mad Mik, only Tailman on sea. What you called?"

"Nel. This is Dida. Are you out of Portland?"

"Go there now. You come along. Be safe."

Dida and Nel stared at each other. That was the last place they wanted to go, but they had no alternative. He nodded at the girl and looked up at the Macaque. "Glad to. We're grateful that you saved our lives."

Mik set about raising his sail. The evening wind, onshore, caught it. They glided smoothly across the dappled waters.

* * * * * * *

184

When Portland came into view, Nel was amazed at the size of the town. When he had been there before, he had not seen anything but the slave pens. That recalled to him those hopeless days. Somehow he had done the impossible, survived his captivity, made his escape. Kept his wits and his life. It seemed almost unreal, now.

Dida seemed nervous as they pulled into the harbor, skirting their way among other vessels, large and small. She squeezed Nel's hand. He understood a bit of what she felt, and he put his arm about her.

The two went unnoticed among the turmoil of the docks—only two more young workers helping a familiar fisherman unload his catch onto a little wheeled cart. They maneuvered it through the milling crowds to the fish market, where Mik haggled with innkeepers and managed to sell the lot for a good price.

Nodding his satisfaction, Mik put the argents into his pouch. "Come 'long," he said, and they followed him to his own quarters. The room was large, with bright rugs on the floor. Tropical patterns decorated the tapestries on the walls.

Mik beamed proudly as he opened a window overlooking the street. "Make good living. Fishing," he said. He took bread and cheese from a cabinet. Other dried foodstuffs were wrapped in paper on the shelves. He set the food on the table and gestured for his guests to help themselves.

They tore into the food with gusto. When they could hold no more, they sat back to talk.

"Is this town always so busy?" asked Dida.

"No," said Mik. "Is Vernal Equ'nox Festival. Soon big party in streets. Night of many lights. Everybody come to Portland for party."

Nel, staring at Dida, was thinking hard. That would be the night of Tarl's raid. "We have to warn the town," he said abruptly.

Dida looked shocked. "They are my own people! I can't betray them!"

Mik stared from one to the other. "Warn who? About what?" he asked, confused.

Nel was intent on Dida. "These are innocent people. If

185

Tarl succeeds, they'll all die, Dida. Like your father and the captains. Have you forgotten? Tarl is even more your enemy than he is mine...or any of those people's." He gestured beyond the window. "Think about it."

She was pale. She shut her round silver eyes and leaned her head on her hands. "I'm a Hawker," she said faintly. Then she looked up suddenly, her gaze harsh. "These aren't my people."

"They're not mine, either. They let me be kept in pens here, remember? They would have let me be sold here as a slave. But I still can't let them be murdered."

"Murd'red? Who be? What you say, Nel?" Mik was standing upright now, his small black eyes bright with anxiety.

Dida seemed to be staring at Nel, but her gaze was turned inward, seeing the head of her father, swinging from the bloodied hand of Tarl. As if reading her mind, Nel said, "Tarl murdered your father. You owe him nothing. We have to warn these people."

Tears filled the silver eyes. Her chin quivered with grief. "Why do things have to be so mixed up and horrible?" she asked.

Nel shook his head. "I don't know. But we have to try and do what's right, just the same. That's one of the things my parents taught me, long ago, and I'll never forget it."

Mik shook the boy's shoulder. "You tell Mik what you mean, or Mik get v'ry angry."

Nel said, "The Seahawks are planning a raid on Portland. On the night when everyone lights candles, they plan to knock out your tower guards and sail right into the bay. Will you help us to warn the militia?"

"Right now!" said the Macaque. He stood up. "You wait here," he said. "Mik go to militia, tell General Tion. Most not listen to Macaque, if they not in towers. Tion diff'rent. You stay, rest, eat. Take time...festival begin tonight. I be back, but probably not soon."

He went out the door, leaving Nel staring at Dida, who stared back. They were in a strange place, and a very strange person had taken upon himself the task of giving the warning.

At last, having eaten everything they could hold, the two sat to watch from the windows as the people of Portland prepared for the beginning of the Vernal Equinox. But Nel found himself thinking, suddenly and strongly, of his mother. He had had little time to think of her recently. She had loved lights. He sighed and turned again to the last of the daylight and the beginning of the night.

* * * * * * *

Mik hurried along the crowded streets. Already some few revelers had lit their candles, and he kept a sharp watch on his tail, which seemed to attract the attention of the rougher sorts, who had already begun their revels. A singed tail meant loss of dignity.

It took longer than he thought it would to reach the barracks. The streets were fuller even than usual, this festival. The thought that it might be on this first night of the celebration that the pirates meant to attack the city made the little Macaque take unusual risks, darting under the necks of riding dogs, slipping between drunken brawlers, putting all of his strength into his dash toward Tion's command quarters.

It grew dark with terrible speed. Ahead, Mik saw the detail assigned to provisioning the watch towers. Finished with the nightly task, the dogriders, led by a lieutenant, were headed back to the barracks. If he delivered the message to them, it would reach headquarters much faster than he could.

Mik dashed up to tug at the trouser-leg of one of the militiamen. "Quick, got message f'r Tion! You take?" he asked, gazing upward in the now-dim light. The man looked down, and Mik saw the terrible scar that marked the face of Slator.

Of all the officers in Portland, he had picked the one least likely to help him! But he was determined to do his best, and he had no idea of Slator's role in the dire plans. "You tell the gen'ral. Hawkers raid Portland...maybe tonight, maybe tomorr'w. While festival go on. Tell Tion." He pitched his voice low, for a panic would, he knew, mean more problem than solution.

Slator grinned down at him, his expression one of amusement. "Arrest this Macaque," he said to the sergeant

187

who rode on his other side. "He is a spy for the renegade Kray. Take him at once to the barracks prison. I will question him later myself."

Mik felt his heart chill beneath his cloak. This man—could this be a conspirator? What terrible fate had led him directly into his clutches? The little Macaque squirmed frantically as he was lifted, bound securely, and taken away.

Shackled, he was locked into the strongest of the detention rooms used by the militia. He felt every minute as it passed, knowing that it could mark the approach of the pirate fleet, but there was nothing that he could do now. It was almost a relief when finally Slator came.

The soldier wasted no time getting to what he wanted to know from Mik. "Who told you about the raid?" That question came again and again. Mik was, as were most of his kind, tough and courageous, and he refused to reply. At last, Slator drew from beneath his cape a flask filled with greenish liquid.

"You refuse to answer, so I am forced to try other means. This may or may not be a fatal dose, but it will bring out of you the information I have to know. Open your mouth, monkey!"

Mik clenched his teeth frantically, but the much larger man held him flat on the floor, pinched his nose shut, and poured in the liquid when the Macaque gasped for breath. It almost strangled him, and he choked and coughed for a long time. When he could breathe, he found that his will was asleep. When Slator asked, he answered, no matter how he strained to keep from doing it. The tale of Nel and Dida came out in a rush. The street where Mik lived, the fact that the two youngsters were still there...all that was revealed in seconds.

Slator grinned, his scar crawling on his narrow face, his eyes as flat and blank as ever. "My thanks," he said mockingly. "Now die, Macaque."

But Mik did not die, even though his belly was on fire and his head swam. He retched, thrusting a finger of a bound hand down his throat, and threw up a good part of the content of his belly. That saved his life, as he had hoped it would.

* * * * * * *

Nel had fallen asleep, though the twinkling of the many lights on the street below had kept Dida interested. When she cried out, however, he snapped into wakefulness.

"What?" he asked groggily.

"Dogriders...there in the street. See in the light of the candles...he's looking up...it's the traitor!"

Nel felt something thud solidly in his chest. He looked down, hoping that she was wrong. Of course, she wasn't. It was the officer who had come to Blood Island. Who could forget that face?

He grabbed Dida by the arm. "Come with me, right now!" Even as the riders pulled to a halt, out of sight at the front of the building, the two crawled onto the ledge outside Mik's window. It wasn't wide, and it was slick with damp, but they clung with fingers and toes to make their way around the corner. There they found a lower roof across a narrow alley, and Nel braced his back against the angle in which a dormer window thrust itself from the wall of his own building.

He heaved, and Dida went flying over and safely down onto the flat span. She gazed up at him, her face a pale and worried triangle. "Be careful," she whispered.

He flung himself into space, feeling the fetid air of the alley flow around his face, the surge of his blood as he pushed himself toward the roof where Dida waited. She caught him as his fingers slid on the slick roof. They didn't speak. Scrambling, they made their way across the rooftop and dropped into the alley on the farther side.

"He'll come after us," whispered Dida urgently, as they peered into the street into which the alleyway led.

"He knows where the barracks is," answered Nel. "We don't. But he doesn't know we don't know. So we'll follow him and let him lead us where we want to go."

They slipped into the crowd on the street and made their way back to the front of Mik's building. The dogs were still tethered there. A commotion above told them that Mik's nice dwelling was getting a very rough going-over. When the riders emerged, led by Slator, whose scarred face was set in grim lines, they mounted at once and set off at a trot along the street.

"It's a good thing he doesn't know what we look like," said Nel. "He was looking for us, there's no doubt of that."

"And Mik?" Dida's voice was almost a whimper.

"Somehow he told the wrong people. We'll find him and help, if we can." Nel concentrated on keeping in sight of the commotion that swirled around the troops' movement down the street.

Was it already too late to carry word to the militia of Portland? Were the pirates even now approaching the harbor over the darkened sea?

* * * * * * *

It had been a festive evening. The general's banquet had been lavish, with wild game from the forest, every sort of fruit and vegetable from the farms about the city, and even mutated turkey, with drumsticks as big as Koola's own leg. He was chewing thoughtfully on the remnant of one of those as he crossed the compound.

The little Macaque was full and happy. He had now had the time to show Gem his city, taking her from the wharves to the palace, where, admittedly, they had only peeped into the ornate gates across the drive. Everywhere they went, the people had received them warmly.

Gem had slipped off to the stables to curry Merry. Koola, feeling a debt to his long-neglected stomach, had tarried to make large inroads into the loaded trays of food. Presently he paused, approaching the row of stables. His Macaque instinct flickered into alertness. He stopped in midstride, head cocked as if listening, but he was feeling far and near with all his senses.

A familiar pattern was teasing his awareness. Light as a feather, a touch tickled at his inner sensing. Something important...but it was too far in the past. He shrugged. Until it became stronger...or went away entirely...there was nothing he could do.

He moved on, passing some troopers beginning to light

the torches around the barracks.

The sun was going down behind the hills.

* * * * * * *

Slator had already dosed the fresh water in the towers with poison. The Macaque there would even now be going into a sleep from which they would never awaken. Tonight the fleet would come into the harbor, and tomorrow he would rule Portland...not with the weak and womanly grasp of his cousin, but with an iron fist that brooked no denial.

He had found the poison in the same place he had obtained the truth-potion—a certain tavern on the dock run by a man who made the stuff from sea-creatures brought in by the nets of fishermen. Slator had found him by accident, when a brawl involving some of his men brought him to the place. He had traded amnesty for his supply of poison, and the tavern keeper had smiled at the swap.

Now, just when everything seemed to be working to plan, two children stood in the way of his ultimate success. Slator was furious. He had to find them! But how was he to recognize, amid the thronging young who now tenanted the streets, two brats he'd never seen?

As he moved around the barracks, Slator tried to scan every face belonging to people of less than adult stature. It occurred to him, then, that he might already have passed them, and he ordered his troop into the street bordering the barracks. He rode the way they had come, searching the faces of everyone they met.

* * * * * * *

Gem looked up from brushing Merry and set the brush aside. "Koola! Full up at last?" She brought the water bucket and set it beside the bearfox. "Here, Merry. Drink up!"

Koola, still gnawing the last of the meat from the bone of the immense turkey leg, looked critically at the animal. "She looking good, Small-boots."

He flung the bone into a barrel of waste and started to speak again. No sound came from his rubbery lips. He

191

looked strange...almost ill.

She stepped to his side. Even as she did, he moaned.
"Koola feel something!"

"What? Are you all right?"

"Is Small-boots' son!" he gasped. "Near. Outside wall...
not far. Danger!"

She stiffened and turned toward the gate. Before Koola
could rise, she was running toward the street. A turbulence in
the crowd up the street caught her attention, and she ran
through the gate toward it. She could see someone struggling
to force a way through the crowd.

Koola, panting up behind, hissed into her ear. "See girl?
She connect with boy! She can tell you where."

Without slowing, she nodded and caught up with the
slight figure of the child, who was still trying to push
through a knot of people. When Gem touched her arm, the
girl whirled, her teeth glinting in a grimace that promised a
fight for whoever bothered her.

"I'm a friend!" said Gem, her tone urgent. "Are you the
girl who knows Nel?"

Round silver eyes stared up, their expression acute, as-
sessing her. Then the child nodded. "We were tryin' to get
word to the militia. Mik went, but he didn't come back, and
that man"—She nodded toward the alley running off at an
angle from the street—"came to Mik's room after he left and
searched it a long time—for us!"

"Word of what?" The woman's voice was almost as
harsh.

"Hawker raid," said the girl, her eyes turning opaque.

"But where's Nel? How did you lose him?"

"Officer chased him in there," said the child, again ges-
turing toward the dark mouth of the alley. "Nel didn't have
any weapon. The officer had a sword."

"I'm Nel's mother," said Gem. "I'll go after them.
Koola, you take care of her." Then she was off running down
the dark cobbles of the alley, skidding in wet and filth.

Once she was into the confusing maze of alleys, Gem
slowed to a walk. Her boots whispered almost soundlessly
over the stones, and she took each corner and angle with as
much caution as if she were again in the forest after bandits.

She avoided the puddles of light at the back doors of shops, holding to shadows as she went toward the sound of a hateful voice that now became audible farther down the alley.

"Now I have you," she heard a cruel voice say clearly.

"What are you going to do?"

The voice was deeper, more assured than she remembered it, but it was *the voice of her son!*

She slipped to the last angle and saw two figures in pool of light from a lamp above a grimy doorway. One of them she recognized immediately as Slator, the evil man Koola had pointed out. The other...

The scar-faced man laughed, a sound like gravel grating over stone. "Don't be foolish, kid. I knew you at once, though I wouldn't have thought to notice you back on Blood Island. The blond boy with the tray, isn't that right? You heard what we said, and you came straight to Portland to destroy my plan."

Nel hefted the sharp-edged pebble he'd caught up when he fell. His mother saw his knuckles turn white with the force of his grasp. She gasped as he flung the stone with all his might, and it ripped across Slator's cheek, leaving a bloody track behind it to match the scar on the other side of his face.

The man put up his fingers. They came away bloody. Nel was now moving backward, out of the light away from the glint of the blade in the soldier's hand.

Slator lunged forward, just as Gem shouted, "Stop that!"

The cry brought him about.

"Leave my son alone, Slator. Face me!"

When Slator saw her, she read his thought in his face: *This is only a woman. How dare she try to interfere with me?* He feinted carelessly, expecting to skewer her on his point. But she wasn't there. Her parry stung him with its strength. He flinched, and then she had him fighting for his life. For the first time in all the long tale of her adventuring she felt what could only be called blood-lust. She recalled what Randor had taught her. She used dazzlingly quick footwork, wheeling around the man, confusing him with feints, nicking him with swift passes.

He grunted and lunged. His blade went through the skin

of her upper arm, and a trickle of blood moved down her sleeve. "First blood!" he exulted, stepping back in the usual way.

Randor's advice, his ancient trick, came into her mind. "First blood means nothing. It's the one who draws last blood that walks away!"

Without hesitation, Gem slashed Slator across the exposed belly, and as he reacted, she used the wrist motion Randor had taught her, and her blade sliced upwards through Slator's neck, cutting his jugular and impaling his neck.

The body hung on her blade. She let the sword with its grisly burden drop as she turned to the boy...who was so much larger than he had been on that terrible morning when she had last seen him.

The boy was staring at her, and she realized that she, too, had changed in vital ways. "Mama?" he asked, sounding almost timid.

She turned to face the light, and the moon, just above the roofs, added its own intensity. They gazed at each other in silence. This was no child. Not any longer. This was a tall, lanky young man, so like her own Nel that it tore at her heart.

They reached for each other and stood clasped together for a long while, both crying and neither caring. They had proved their courage.

"I thought you were dead, like Pa," the boy said, awe in his voice.

"I almost was," she said. "But I lived. It's all right now...we're together again. Things are going to be fine. Now."

He gasped. as if remembering something important. "Maybe not! I've got to get to somebody who can do something, Mama!"

"General Tion," she said. "Come with me, son."

They ran back up the alley together, their boots sounding a triumphant clamor against the ancient stones.

* * * * * * *

General Tion was tired. It had been a day full of activity,

ending in his festival dinner. Now his guests had gone, and he was sitting in his chair, listening to his wife move about as she directed the servants in clearing away the mess in the big dining room.

The clatter of heels on cobblestones reluctantly brought him to his front door to stare into the torch-lit yard of the officers' quarters. The shout of the guard at the gate was still ringing in the air as he saw that the newcomer was Gem. Beside her ran a tall blond boy so like her that he knew it must be her son.

It took a moment to tell Nel's story. Tion was no laggard when an emergency arose. Aides went flying in all directions with orders for the troops. Dogriders were sent to the docks, followed by foot soldiers armed with rockets. Tion himself set out for the tower nearest the barracks, mounted on his fastest dog.

Before he arrived there, he found Koola riding at elbow. Gem was mounted behind the Macaque, riding double on Koola's commandeered Airedale. They were riding too fast for talk. Tion, however, suspected that they, too, rode with cold dread chilling the pits of their stomachs. The faithful Macaques had manned the towers for many years, and never had the Hawkers raided Portland. What would they find when they came to the guard post?

It was worse than anything he could have imagined. All the watchers in the near tower were dead, sprawled amid their own vomit, stiffening in the cold night air. Tion felt sick himself. Such faithful duty as the monkey-men had rendered should not be rewarded with death.

"Who provisioned the towers tonight?" he asked the sergeant who had followed him with a small detachment of troopers.

"Slator," said the sergeant, his tone grim.

"If you hadn't killed him, I would have," the general said to Gem. He turned to the sergeant. "Order the bombards loaded with mid-weight ball. Put troops on the vessels anchored in the harbor, and order them to lie low until they see the rockets. We are going to surprise some Seahawks tonight."

CHAPTER NINETEEN

Tarl stood at the bow of the lead vessel. Behind him came the united strength of the Seahawk fleet. His snaggled teeth showed in a grin, even in the darkness of the night. The moon was just coming up over the mainland, and against the backdrop of dark forest and hills Portland shone with pinpricks of yellow light.

Tarl laughed softly. Soon enough, that revelry would be lost in blood. Soon enough, he would be master of Portland, wealthy beyond any dream with the loot of that fat city. And Slator...he laughed harder, though to himself, to think of the expectations of that traitor. Slator would hang by the heels until Tarl consented to let him die.

He looked back at the great ships whispering across the heaving waves. Dark-sailed, without lamps at their bowsprits, they seemed like ghosts...or demons...as they slipped toward their unsuspecting prey. An unconscious sigh left the pirate's lips as he turned again toward the city, where the beacons on the towers seemed to beckon their oncoming destruction.

Tarl's lead ship crept between the headlands. There was no sign of life in the towers on either hand. Sounds of merriment came to his ears from the town across the bay, but the docks were pitch-dark. He stared at the nearest of the towers. The beacons burned steadily, but it was quiet....as a grave. He grunted.

Clearly, Slator had done his work well.

Chukker, just behind him, nudged his shoulder. That meant that the last of the ships had cleared the entrance to the bay. Tarl gestured, and a torch-basket was hoisted on the signal mast.

196

They would be ready to come about and ease up to the docks very soon, now. He stepped up to stand beside the man at the wheel. "Hard over," he breathed into an unwashed ear, and the man obeyed, turning the wheel put the ship about....

Then the sky burst into red and orange as rockets roared into the sky, stringing behind them tails of fire. One arched over Tarl's ship to take the next in line in its mainsail. The crash echoed over the water, and a projectile splintered the side of a third pirate vessel.

Mouth open with astonishment, Tarl saw torches spring to life along the docks. Catapults were outlined against their glare, and men with bows were bringing hisses of arrows to bear on the encroaching pirate fleet. Tarl heard Chukker, who had been yelling something inarticulate, gurgle. The man fell across the rail, struggled there for moment, then pitched into the bay.

Frozen in horror and surprise, Tarl watched the destruction of his fleet. Around him his own ship was burning. Men leaped onto the docks, only to be skewered on swords or spitted on arrows. He wanted to move, to do something to halt this terrible disaster, but he couldn't.

He was standing, yet when the ship sank in shallow water. He didn't try to swim, and he drowned quietly, without a struggle.

* * * * * * *

Gem, standing on the hill beside one of the towers with Tion and his officers, held Nel's hand in one of her own and Dida's in the other. She had thought that she would be fiercely happy to see the destruction of the pirates who had killed her man. She had expected to exult, to shout, to laugh, as the awful comedy played itself out.

She found that she was only sick and sad. Dida, beside her, was crying silently, tears spilling from the silver eyes. Death was death, no matter who suffered it. There was no glory in it for anyone, whatever the cause. Only in life could there be glory.

Below, the ships were sinking or burning or floating aimlessly on the disturbed waves. Arrows still flew, but they were growing fewer. The battle was over, and Portland was safe. She thought of the strange twists of fate that had brought her here, together with her son and this child of pirates, at the time and in the place where they could do the most good for many people. If this had not been true, Portland might have died on this Festival night.

Randor had known how she would feel, she thought. He was the one who had taught her the danger of fighting to destroy, instead of to defend. "It destroys the one who lives that way," he had told her. She could see in this bay the truth of that.

Dida, watching the deaths of her people, was now sobbing. Gem turned and put her arms about the child, but Dida struggled free and faced the bay again.

A last ship was moving toward the dock, its rails lined with armed men. They sprang from the burning ship onto the dock into a wall of arrows. Many fell, but those left alive stormed into that hail like heroes.

"Show 'em!" Dida yelled suddenly. "Show 'em how Hawkers die!" Then she was again in Gem's arms, and Nel was patting her awkwardly on her shoulder.

It was finished now. For all of them.

* * * * * * *

Portland was delirious with relief. Added to the joy of the Festival, the victory over the Hawkers was almost intoxicating.

Only General Tion was worried. He had two hundred captive Hawkers on his hands, and he had no facilities for imprisoning them. He had them in the compound, guarded, but he didn't like it. And he didn't quite know how to solve the problem.

Gem visited him early. She had put her wits to work. "Why don't you do what Kenteen did...make them swear allegiance to the King? Then let them go?"

"It's a matter of their keeping their word. I doubt they'd do it, and then we'd be in a pickle again," he replied.

"You saved a lot of the ships, didn't you?"

"Yes."

"Then put them in charge of a navy!"

"Official pirates?" He sounded shocked.

"No, sailors. Traders, up and down the coast, tying all the little places together in commerce."

Tion stared. "They could also defend us from any other pirate bands that might spring up," he breathed. "I think you're some sort of military genius!"

Late that afternoon, Nel brought a bit of information that fitted exactly into the plan. "Bolton is alive!" he cried, as he ran up to his mother and the general, who by now had heard his whole story.

The two adults stared over his head at each other. "How do you know?" Gem asked.

"A Hawker that Dida and I were working on—with the medics, you know—told us he is still on the Island. Chained. Tarl intended to torture him to death, after the raid."

Gem's eyes sparkled. "Probably the one man who can make your navy work is Bolton. You might send someone out to see what he thinks about the idea."

For two days Nel haunted the docks, while his mother spent time with Dida. He was pleased that the two liked each other. It was certain that neither was the stay-at-home sort. It pleased him even more that Gem had asked the girl to go with them when they went back to join First Dog and Cormal. The girl had hesitated for only a moment. Then she had agreed, with the proviso that she could come back to Portland if she didn't like the forest lands.

Gem and Dida found Nel at the docks when they needed his help to hunt for their two errant Macaques. Mik—now a bit of a hero himself—and Koola seemed to get into more scrapes than their friends could keep them out of.

They asked along the streets until someone directed them to a tavern. The proprietor pointed to a corner table. "If those belong to you, I'll gladly pay you ten argents to take them away," he said plaintively.

Koola and Mik slept amid a clutter of empty mugs. On both faces were identical idiotic grins.

* * * * * * *

Nel's vigil ended the next morning when a boat carrying Bolton pulled up at the dock. The old man spotted Nel at once. "So you made it, lad!" he shouted.

"And found my mother, too!" Nel held out a hand and hauled the one-legged man onto the dock. General Tion had come along, and Nel turned to him. "This is the general, and he sent for you," he told Bolton.

Bolton looked the general over as thoroughly as Tion was studying the old pirate. Then Bolton thrust out a hand. Tion took it.

"Your man who fetched me said something about starting up a navy," Bolton said in greeting.

"A real fleet, sanctioned, supplied, and supported by the township of Portland," the general said.

"Good for your people, but what about mine?"

"They'll be paid for all services. Your fleet will be rebuilt by the best boat-builders in Portland. New ones, too, built to your specifications," the general said.

Bolton rubbed his bald head. "We'd still base on the island?"

"No. A fleet would have to be based in the harbor."

"Trapped in that bay? You've got to keep a fleet maneuverable. It's got to be able to put to sea, no matter what. And my folk wouldn't rest easy cheek-by-jowl with yours. Nor yours with mine, I'd wager."

The general stroked his jaw. "There's sense in that. I'm no sailor."

"I am. If we're to make a navy, it must be done my way."

The general grinned. "Welcome aboard, Admiral," he said.

Bolton looked stunned for a moment. Then he beamed. He turned to Nel. "You going to sign on, lad?"

"Not right now, Bolton. Maybe one day. I like the sea, but for now I want to be with my mother for a while. But I know a fine mate, if you need one. A Macaque named Mik. He saved Dida and me from drowning."

"A Macaque? That's the craziest thing I ever heard!"

"Crazy as Bolton One-leg being Admiral of the King's Navy?"

200

Bolton whooped with laughter. "Now, would ye just say that title again?"

EPILOGUE

The patrol on its way to rejoin First Dog came to Dover in early summer. The excited villagers poured from houses and shops and fields to meet the troops.

Gem, at the head of the column beside the captain, was followed by Nel, Dida, and Koola, along with twenty fresh riders. One was the chaplain Kenteen had asked for.

Gem saw her mother moving through the crowd. She sprang from Merry's back and ran to greet her.

Bere looked from her daughter to her grandson, her eyes still bright and wise. "Well, you did it," she said proudly, her eyes brimming. "You came back, and with Little Nel, too. Good work."

She looked up at the big boy atop the riding dog. "You've grown a mite since I saw you, boy. Come down and hug me."

Nel sprang down and embraced his grandmother. Dida waited until he nodded and did the same. Bere didn't turn a hair. In time, Bere drew Gem aside. "I must tell you something, Daughter."

"There's a lot I need to tell you, but there will never be time."

"You're not going to stay?" Bere stared into Gem's eyes. "You've met somebody...who will take Big Nel's place?"

Gem nodded. "Cormal is his name. I'll tell you all about him when we're alone tonight. I need to go out to see Randor, now."

"Gem, that's what I needed to tell you. Randor's gone."

"How?"

"Hunting a rock-cat that killed Dolan's girl. He hunted

202

alone, always, you know."

Gem nodded. That was his way, she knew. She felt tears form in her eyes.

"They found him in the snow, almost clawed to bits. Brought him to me, and I did what I could. But it was too late."

"Did he...suffer?" Gem asked.

"He was pretty numb by then. But he gave me a message for you. Seemed certain you'd come back."

Gem was staring at her mother.

"He said you weren't to mourn him. He said that he's going to the next one. Do you know what he might have meant by that?" Bere looked puzzled.

Her daughter sighed. "He used to tell me stories about his adventures. I asked him, one night, which of all of them was the best and most exciting." She smiled faintly, remembering. "He said that was easy. It's always the next one!"

Bere kissed her on the cheek. "They buried him in his woods, near his house. I'll show you, if you like."

"We'll take flowers," said Gem. "He saved me, more than once. I thought of him, what he'd do, how he'd handle things, so often."

Bere smiled. "You made him proud, child. You were his last pupil."

www.ingramcontent.com/pod-product-compliance
Lightning Source LLC
Chambersburg PA
CBHW032006240626
47153CB00003B/1140